About Apollo Africa

The original Heinemann African Writers Series was launched in 1962 with the publication of Chinua Achebe's *Things Fall Apart*, Cyprian Ekwensi's *Burning Grass* and Kenneth Kaunda's *Zambia Shall Be Free*, with Achebe himself acting as an editorial advisor. Over the next 40 years, the series continued to publish the best writing from across the African continent.

One of the founding aims of the Heinemann series was to make books by African writers available to as wide a readership as possible. Apollo Africa – a collaboration between Black Star Books and Head of Zeus – is proud to continue this work, ensuring novels, essays, poetry and plays from the original series are once again made available to readers all over the world.

Sugarcane with Salt

Sugarcane with Salt

James Ng'ombe

Black Star Books and Head of Zeus would like to thank the following organisations: The Miles Morland Foundation, The Ford Foundation, and Africa No Filter. This publication was made possible through their support.

First published in the Longman African Writers Series in 1989 by Pearson Education Limited

This edition first published in the UK in 2024 by Head of Zeus Ltd, part of Bloomsbury Publishing Plc.

Copyright © James Ng'ombe, 1989

The moral right of James Ng'ombe to be identified as the author of this work has been asserted in accordance with the Copyright, Designs and Patents Act of 1988.

All rights reserved. No part of this publication may be reproduced, stored in a retrieval system, or transmitted in any form or by any means, electronic, mechanical, photocopying, recording, or otherwise, without the prior permission of both the copyright owner and the above publisher of this book.

This reprint is published by arrangement with Pearson Education Limited.

This is a work of fiction. All characters, organizations, and events portrayed in this novel are either products of the author's imagination or are used fictitiously.

9 7 5 3 1 2 4 6 8

A catalogue record for this book is available from the British Library.

ISBN (PB): 9781035900749
ISBN (E): 9781803288390

Typeset by Siliconchips Services Ltd UK

Printed and bound in Great Britain by
CPI Group (UK) Ltd, Croydon CR0 4YY

Head of Zeus Ltd
First Floor East
5–8 Hardwick Street
London EC1R 4RG

WWW.HEADOFZEUS.COM

Chapter One

Khumbo stepped into the September sun, now throwing its rays fiercely, but threatened by heavy, dark clouds around it. He knew though that the rains were still a whole month or so away, and that the bush fires must already have forced hundreds of mice from their underground hideouts into the hands of the scheming and salivating herdboys. The first rain, *zimalupsya*, when it came, brought with it an aura of ecstasy as expectant mothers rushed out in search of anthill soil which they sucked to satisfy the insatiable greed of the new life within them. Those who didn't have an anthill in sight – although they would not give up looking for this most treasured delicacy delivered by the spirits from underneath through the medium of ants – those who had to look for alternatives, went for the mudwalls of the house, kitchen or *nkhokwe*, and extracted a lump or two. Khumbo had always wondered as a boy why his mother ate so much rubbish to fill an already full stomach. As for the boys, it was the crickets, the grasshoppers and the mice that came with the tilling of the steaming soil which brought about prospects of excitement. Without these they considered turning the soil upside down the worst form of punishment any parent could inflict on childhood.

Khumbo felt warm inside, more so when he heard his name called from the balcony. It was Billy. He waved back, after putting down his luggage, overwhelmed by a surge of genuine happiness. It was good to be home. It was good to be surrounded by a sea of black faces without fear of Brixton riots or being mugged at an underground station. It was good to be able to see clearly for miles and miles around this flat city, the new capital. The stretch of flatness always amazed him. It was good for farming; he remembered his secondary school geography and why the prairies were greatest for wheat-farming. Tractors and other machinery could work on flat land, not on hilly or rocky surfaces. Consequently Lilongwe, the capital of the country, had also come to represent the centre of estate farming – tobacco, maize and cattle. He picked up his luggage and disappeared into the immigration room. He was so lost in thoughts about Billy, home and the radiant sun that he did not pay attention to the special scrutiny his passport was receiving from the immigration officer. Feeling sweat rolling down his armpits, he wondered whether it had always been this hot. He gave up and left the question to dissolve in the armpit sweat.

'You have been away eight years,' the officer started in Chichewa, seemingly amused.

'Yes,' Khumbo replied absent-mindedly.

'That's a long time,' pursued the officer.

'Yes,' he mumbled in his absent-mindedness.

'Doing what?'

'Studying.'

The officer looked at the passport again and then at Khumbo before stamping it and handing it back to him.

'You will report at the Training Office,' concluded the officer.

'Why?' Khumbo asked, suddenly attentive.

'Who sent you overseas?' asked the officer.

'The Government.'

'How does the Government know you are back then?'

'I see,' said Khumbo as he lifted his luggage to proceed to the customs desk. Actually he didn't see the officer's point. Khumbo knew better than to press the officer for elaboration. He would find out at the Training Office anyway.

The searching through his luggage by the customs officer was thorough but the length of his stay abroad cleared him of any duty.

'You can go, Mr Dala,' said the customs officer.

'Thank you,' Khumbo answered, loading his trolley.

He pushed the trolley into the crowd waiting for arrivals. Billy pulled it from the front. They shook hands vigorously as soon as they were clear of the crowd.

'*Ada*,' they chorused in unison. They preferred *ada* to the usual *achimwene*. They had always been the best of friends.

'How are you?' enquired Billy.

'I am fine, thanks. And you?'

'*Bo, ada, Bo.*' Hearing Billy talk *Bo* lifted Khumbo to heights of enjoyment he hadn't known for some time.

'Where is everybody?' Khumbo asked.

'I'll explain in the car.'

Khumbo smelt the alcohol. Billy wasn't actually staggering, but it wasn't difficult to notice his slovenly appearance or the lazy slur in his speech. His eyes: something about him he couldn't explain yet.

'Okay, let's see the yellow submarine,' Khumbo agreed, quoting one of Billy's letters.

It turned out to be a Renault 16.

Clearing the unaccompanied luggage took them a whole hour. It was as if the heat had reduced every action to slow motion. He heard the noise the fan made but could only sympathise with the well-meaning intention behind its purchase. It would take a dozen of them to have any impact. As soon as they set off in Billy's car, Khumbo realised that the Renault was running on God's mercy. The speedometer was not functioning and the upholstery was in need of repair. The tyres were quite a sight in their threadbare smoothness, not to mention the coughing from under the bonnet. After trying the starter for the fourth time, the car cough came through. Khumbo was forced to take a second look at his brother, easily taller and sturdier than himself. His face, marked by the popping red eyes and the creeping baldness, was essentially buried in a free-growing beard. A Jonas Savimbi face,

Khumbo thought. A face that gave him a military – if not mercenary – appearance. A face toughened by realities of death and gunsmoke in a war that would eventually only benefit the scheming arms dealers. A face ageing from the uncertainties of a future after a war in which brother fought brother and children knew no parents.

Billy drove looking fixedly ahead, as if concentrating on struggling with the ill-aligned wheels. Khumbo, for his part, did not have anything to say. He just looked on, marvelling at the expanse of land to the left and to the right as they embarked on the thirty-minute drive to the city. Acacia trees lined the road to Lilongwe. In fact, as he discovered later, acacia and gmelina were the adopted trees in the 'Keep the city green' campaign that surrounded the transfer of the government headquarters from Zomba to Lilongwe.

'Did you have a car in London?' Billy asked.

'Yes.' Khumbo answered.

'Are you bringing it in?' Billy continued.

'No, Sue will need it.' Sue was Khumbo's girlfriend in England. 'In any case, it's an old car.'

'Listen,' Billy said, now turning to face him fully, momentarily scaring his brother with this distraction from his driving. Then he faced the road again.

'You are back home. Here, age of a car does not matter. What you need is a loan-free car. Only companies and Asians – well, and big timers too – can afford new cars. Those who can are bringing their cars from overseas.'

'Well, it wasn't necessary, really,' ventured Khumbo in his defeat, hoping he wouldn't have to defend his stance any further.

'Three months, *ada*,' Billy concluded. 'I'm giving you three months. Let's see what you will be saying then.'

The first fifteen minutes did not bring into view anything worth noting. But in the following ten to fifteen minutes they drove through an industrial area with factories and silos on the left. He particularly noticed the Coca-Cola factory and the maize silos on the right. The big white buildings on the right housed the National Teacher Training College. Beyond it, he was told, was the Lilongwe train station. The rail line had been extended from Salima to Lilongwe and had continued all the way to Mchinji on the Malawi-Zambia border. Then came the National Police Headquarters just before area 18, the high-density residential area popular for its endless supply of secretaries and single women. You just didn't mention a visit to area 18 to your wife and expect supper that evening. In all this Billy played the role of a tour guide very well.

At a roundabout they turned left into Presidential Way to the city centre in search of petrol. Khumbo had no idea where they were as they pulled up by a filling station.

'Two Kwacha,' Billy shouted as he pulled two notes from his jacket. Then he turned to Khumbo, 'How is she?'

'She is all right,' Khumbo said evasively.

'Tell me about her.'

'Oil check, sir?' asked the petrol attendant, and went

ahead following a non-committal grunt from Billy who was then forced to pull the bonnet cord.

'You need at least a pint, sir,' he shouted from inside the bonnet.

'Next time,' Billy shouted back.

'Put in a pint,' Khumbo intervened and felt for his wallet. Pound notes flashed out.

'Wait a minute,' Khumbo cautioned the attendant. And then to Billy: 'Can you pay and I'll give it back to you after I've changed my pounds?'

'Okay.'

'Two pints,' shouted Khumbo to the attendant.

'I don't have that much, *ada*,' Billy protested. 'One pint!' He altered the instruction.

Khumbo had questions to ask, misgivings to express about the car, everything, everybody, but thought better of it. Soon the car was back to its coughing as they sped down the main road back Presidential Way. Lilongwe had changed beyond recognition in the eight years he had been abroad. It was now the capital city. All government ministries had already transferred from Zomba. Well, all but the Parliament, which meant the MPs and civil servants travelling 200 miles down to Zomba anytime Parliament was in session. Good business for the hotels in Blantyre and Zomba! The airport itself, three times the size of Chileka Airport in Blantyre, was an isolated but impressively modern complex by any standard. New high- and low-density residential areas had cropped up. And they turned into area 18. The locations were just known by area numbers. From the top of the street the green roofing merged into one sheet spreading over miles. They were now on a street full of casual pedestrians walking to and from nowhere. After taking several turns, the car finally came to a halt outside a semi-detached house, surrounded by hundreds of similar houses. '*Ada*, this is area 18,' Billy announced. 'And this here is Mr Billy Dala's palace.' Then he stepped out of the car.

'Welcome home!'

'Thank you,' Khumbo said as soon as he got out, yawning and stretching, enjoying the sounds of his bones cracking. There was a big truck parked on the road, and they had parked just in front of it as there was no drive or carport at the house. Car owners either had to park on the street or construct little bridges across the water drain if they wished to park their cars by their houses. Billy did the latter. Billy's neighbour came round to help with the luggage and Khumbo thought he and Billy would manage. So he disappeared into the house, away from the gaze of the neighbours and the questioning looks of their children. Some followed him to the house, keeping a safe distance of course, but always muttering something about him, his trip and the suit he was wearing, or the suitcase, which they considered of a special quality. He took the liberty of surveying the house – two bedrooms, a kitchen, toilet, shower and sitting-room – with rooms without any special design; boxes really. But this was in keeping with the design of the houses in the location – box design. This is where all civil servants started their toil up the bureaucratic ladder. Perhaps ten years later, maybe twenty, they would deserve a house in area 11, 12 or 13, one which had servants' quarters, four bedrooms, two bathrooms, a shower and a garage. That might require a stroke of luck, more likely it would require special knowledge of some big shot. He proceeded to the bedroom. The bed was not made, and there were trousers, shirts and jackets hanging everywhere, mostly on the lines knotted between a burglar bar on the window and the ventilator on the opposite wall. As a result the line sagged with weight to the extent that Khumbo had to walk close to the wall in order to walk upright. There were some female items here and there, some of them intimate. He took in one last detail: his brother might be untidy, but he sure had expensive tastes. The furniture, kitchen items and clothes had cost him some money. He took in all these details against a background of laughter and chatter from Billy and his friend as they brought in the suitcases, they too commenting on the quality of this, the weight of that, etc. He returned to the sitting-room as soon as they had completed their task.

'*Ada*, this is Sam,' Billy said as Khumbo was about to go into the other room where his suitcases had been deposited. 'Sam Mateyo.' And then, as Khumbo drew closer and stretched out his arm, 'And this stranger here is my one and only brother, Khumbo Dala. Pardon me, Dr Khumbo Dala.'

'I am pleased, Mr Mateyo,' Khumbo said, shaking Sam's hand.

'I am pleased to know you – I've heard lots about you.'

A man wearing overalls entered carrying the biggest and heaviest suitcase.

'This is Jomo,' Billy said. 'My truck driver.'

'Your...?' Khumbo did not complete the question. He just shook Jomo's coarse and strong hand and watched him go out.

'We call him Jomo because of his belt, and size of course, like Jomo Kenyatta,' Billy explained.

'Call me Sam, if you don't mind,' Sam offered. 'It's easier.'

'Of course, of course. Drop the Doctor business and call me Khumbo. I'm sure you will also find that easier.'

And that marked the beginning of laughter, drinking and story-telling. The three of them sat in easy chairs and let the hi-fi complement the social atmosphere. The sitting-room served as a dining-room as well. The big refrigerator in the kitchen corner was full of beer and nothing else. Jomo called Billy outside once and a few minutes later Khumbo heard the truck roar off.

'Shall we go for lunch?' suggested Sam an hour later. If Sam didn't watch it he would soon look like a drum supported by two sticks. Obesity would be the word for it.

'Where?' enquired Khumbo, still anxious to ask about the truck, but holding back, preferring to discuss it strictly as a family matter.

'We are having lunch at Sam's place,' Billy explained. 'You see, Sam is married…'

'So are you Billy…' Sam wasn't allowed to finish.

'Shut up!' Billy flared up, his big oval mouth releasing a squirt.

'You? Married and you never told me?' Khumbo asked, aghast.

'I am sorry, Billy,' said Sam apologetically. 'I didn't mean to…'

As Billy's eyes blazed, he stroked and pulled at his beard with a distant look in his eyes.

'Of course you ought to tell him yourself.'

'That's all we'll say on the matter.' Billy stood up with an air of finality, his gigantic body towering over the seated two. It was as if the outburst had suddenly explained and justified his physical dominance.

Khumbo had seen the fear in Sam's eyes – and of course the ferocity in Billy had not been lost on him – and could not believe his brother's naked brutality. Within the hour he had known Sam, he had seemed a nice guy, just looking for company and fun in life. All Sam wanted, it seemed to Khumbo, was good food, drink and company. How could anyone shout at a friend who had offered a meal – the first meal to be offered to his brother on his return? Sam also stood up, dazed more by the frozen atmosphere than the liquor. He was not as big as Billy; in fact he was nearly the same height as Khumbo, except for his bulging tummy and light skin.

What had got into Billy? The beer now tasted stale, and Khumbo was genuinely lost – as lost as the needle which mother chicken is still looking for in the sand as she scratches and pecks at the soil, scratching and pecking in spite of the decree from the oracle that the needle was doomed to eternal darkness inside the all-conquering earth.

'Okay, everybody,' Sam said, in an attempt to restore the atmosphere to its earlier warmth. 'Let's go and eat.'

'Okay,' Khumbo agreed. 'I can't wait.'

'Have you told him about the party?' enquired Sam of Billy.

'No,' answered Billy rather curtly. 'Tell him,' he ordered.

'We are having a party tonight.' Sam told Khumbo.

'Oh! That sounds exciting,' said Khumbo as he went out ahead of Billy to join Sam, leaving his brother to lock the door.

'Well,' Sam went on, 'we have to celebrate the big day, man.'

'What big day?'

They both burst into big laughter as they approached Sam's house. Billy followed, right hand in his pocket, left hand pulling at the beard.

The party was a success, judging by the number of guests who turned up, the number of girls who came unaccompanied, and the number of bottles going around.

After lunch Khumbo had retired to his room for a siesta

which had lasted until dusk. When he staggered back to the sitting-room he could see crates in the kitchen. Later he learned that Sam and Billy had spent most of the afternoon transferring the crates from Sam's house and then setting up the stereo for the evening. That explained the noise. He cracked his knuckles, something he enjoyed after waking from sleep when the bones were laziest.

Khumbo opened a beer and drained it in several gulps. He opened another and sat in the chair next to the door, waiting for whatever the evening had in store for him at the get-together. He cracked his knuckles again and this time they hurt. He watched disinterestedly the loitering chickens, dogs and children mingling freely and throwing furtive glances every now and then in his direction. He was by now used to being a curiosity in the location. Now, the fatigue and drowsiness he felt after the sleep worsened his drunken state and increased his oblivion towards the noisy neighbourhood. He was already adjusting to the free mixing between man and his immediate natural environment – chickens, pets, cabbages. You wake up one morning and discover that a neighbour's chicken has lain an egg in your flour basket. You don't complain, you don't inherit it. You report the event to the owner and between the owner and yourself you work out the best way of accommodating the bird during this most profitable period. In any case your neighbour's chicken might save you on a day when you have nothing with which to entertain your guests.

It wasn't until the party was over that Billy and Khumbo had time to discuss family matters. They sat opposite each other, each holding a beer bottle rather ceremoniously, each discovering in the other the stranger that had replaced his childhood brother in the years that had passed. And yet each not very comfortable about the prospects of getting to know the stranger.

'You are the only one who has been answering my letters these past few years,' Khumbo said uneasily, but believing that was as good a starting point as any.

'I enjoy reading about those far places,' Billy answered evasively. 'You see, now that we have our own university it takes so much to justify training abroad. With my administration diploma, I have very little hope of doing what you have done. But one of these days I intend to see the world. On my own.'

'What about the parents?' asked Khumbo.

'Mother has never been much of a writer.'

'But Baba used to…' Khumbo insisted. Billy looked at him with blazing eyes, his heavy trunk breathing laboriously, the discomfiture resulting from a mixture of drink, fatigue and Khumbo's questions.

'*Ada*, it was all right when you lived far away,' Billy started. 'There are things which have been happening. Nobody was brave enough to write you.'

'What things?' Khumbo blurted, instinctively cracking his knuckles, for once assuming his rightful role as the elder. 'I'm part of it, you know… I hate to be treated like an outsider.'

There were things he didn't understand all right. But that's why he was asking questions. New things like the *chamba* being smoked freely at the party.

'Father and mother don't live together any more.' Billy stopped and waited for the cloud of silence and shock to lift somewhat.

'What are you saying?'

'Paweme is working in Blantyre – as a secretary.' He took a long gulp from the bottle before continuing, his thick beard rocking with the gulps. 'She is the only one of your sisters who made it. Ellen lives with Paweme in Blantyre – doing odd clerical jobs here and there. Now that is the story.'

'That doesn't sound like much of a story to me,' continued Khumbo in his aggressive mood. 'There is something you are hiding…' He checked himself and rephrased the question. 'Is that all, *ada*? What do you mean Baba and mother don't live together? I mean, what's happening? What about Chimwemwe?'

'Look here, brother…' Billy said as he rose from the chair and staggered towards the window, unable to complete his sentence. He was fighting a strong impulse to just explode and let everything out. He placed the bottle on the window and looked out into the darkness, a darkness which bore no evidence of the hectic party that had ended an hour earlier. In fact in a couple of hours the eastern horizon would be clearing. In the uneasiness that followed, Khumbo too rose to his feet and walked to the toilet. A minute later he flushed it and walked out, except that he stopped half-way through the room.

'I may be asking difficult questions *ada*,' he said. But I have to ask them, and you are the only one around to answer them. You are the only one I can be frank with. We have never kept anything from each other.'

Billy still preferred to look out into the dark.

'I was glad when you wrote about Sue. I thought you would not come back. Now you ask about Chimwemwe. What am I to make of this?'

'Sue and I are not married. And I have to ask about Chimwemwe. You know that very well.'

Billy picked up the bottle and turned round.

'Now that you are here, it's best that you find out the truth about the family. But on your own. Tomorrow take my car and go home.' He checked himself. 'What home? We never were home people really. But Baba is in the same place, same town.' He attempted a laugh and failed miserably.

'I guess that's what I'll have to do.' Khumbo sighed as he slumped back into his chair.

'I don't remember when I last visited the village,' Billy offered. 'They talked about us, you know. Our education, how it has spoiled us. How it has destroyed the family. Uncle Jumbe...' He stopped and walked towards the bedroom.

'Come on, let's use the remaining few hours. That's your room.'

Khumbo went into his room but didn't undress, and therefore saw no need of turning over the blankets. After all, if he had a choice he would have preferred the cool morning breeze outside to the humidity inside the blanket.

Left to his thoughts, back in the waiting-room, Khumbo used the occasion to reminisce on the brief encounter with the Chief Training Officer. Everything had gone wrong. He couldn't find his file, you see his secretary never brought him the right files, had never done it in the three years she had worked for him. Hung above the senior official, in its immaculateness, was the portrait of the Head of State, symbolising discipline and efficiency at work in decision making and implementation, and public relations, both on the domestic and international scene. And yet immediately below this symbol stood a Mr Chete, a cheap mockery of all that the portrait symbolised, an inferior imitation of the ultimate in the hierarchy of efficiency. To the Chetes, the caricature of a smiling secretary was all the buffer they needed against embarrassment and exposure. One wondered how many of those smiling faces went home at the end of the day uncertain if they would return to their offices tomorrow; for their efficiency, if ill timed, would suffer their superiors irreparable damage should the exposure take place in the presence of some of their bosses. Indeed, one had to learn the game of shielding such ineptitude if one was to survive in one's post as a secretary.

'Dr Dala.' Flossie, Mr Chete's secretary, interrupted his thoughts.

'There's a call for you.' He rushed in. 'Take it on that one.'

'*Ada!*' it was Billy.

'*Ada!*'

'How is it going?' Billy enquired.

'Nothing doing,' Khumbo started cautiously, but then decided he might as well tell it all. 'I don't know if I have a file or not. At one time they are ready to see me. Next thing I know about it the man had called for a wrong file. Apologies, etc.'

'Have you already seen the man?' Billy asked.

'Literally, yes. But nothing else.'

'Then what are you waiting for?'

'I've been told to wait until they have found the file.' Billy laughed, first loudly and then in a low tone.

'I don't find that funny... and I made the mistake of wearing tweed. You should see the sweat...'

He caught Flossie giggling and through his dramatic face made a point about his not being amused by her encroachment into his private conversation.

'Listen, I wish I had explained before leaving the house,' Billy added apologetically.

'Explained what?'

'Just ask when you can come back,' continued Billy, 'I'll explain the rest at home.' And as Khumbo was about to hang up, Billy screamed into the mouthpiece, 'and don't show them that you are impatient. See you later.' They hung up.

Khumbo debated the wisdom of going to Mr Chete just to find out when he should come back, especially in view of Billy's phone call.

'Do you think he will see me today, before lunch?' He enquired of Flossie.

'I doubt it,' she said as she opened the door to Mr Chete's office. 'Let me find out.'

The door closed behind her. A minute later she was back. 'Give us two weeks. And then report straight to the Ministry of Health Headquarters.'

Khumbo walked out without a 'thank you' or a 'goodbye', seeing no justification for either. As he walked on to the pavement he cracked his knuckles, loosened his necktie and took off his jacket, which he flung on his shoulder. When he got to the car he threw the jacket and necktie on to the back seat. He let the car roar off and thoroughly enjoyed the noise thus created. He lowered both front windows to let in breeze and cool down the high temperature inside the car.

He had an hour before lunch, and so he naturally found himself at the Capital Hotel, quenching his thirst and the morning's frustrations in a glass of beer. The Capital Hotel was the biggest in Lilongwe and had been built with heavy Danish investment. Unlike most African hotels which modelled themselves on big names in the west by building skyscrapers, Capital Hotel, if approached from Capital Hill, was a fine and romantic spread of red brick and tile ending in a shape that was quadrilateral. It was surrounded by trees and shrubs which denied passers-by easy visual access to the inner activities. You had to drive in to get the full impact of the red building at close range. The floor and doors were green. These are Capital colours: green and red-brown really because red brick is essentially brown in colour. He walked past the reception through the upper lounge and down the steps to the bar and called for Carlsberg, the Danish beer brewed locally – by the only Carlsberg plant on the continent. Or so the company boasted. He knew nobody around and therefore spent the next hour alone. Just before noon he returned to the office for Billy and Sam.

'You're both invited to lunch with me – in style,' Khumbo offered. He was feeling very generous now that he had changed his sterling travellers' cheques into Kwacha.

'I don't see much alternative to that. So we are all yours.' Billy was in jovial and frivolous mood, which was quite a change from yesterday.

Sam, on the other hand, was contemplative and moody, joining a conversation only to correct or add a point. At the hotel they treated themselves to the Carlsberg commonly known as 'green' – hence the advertisement 'Give a Guy a Green' now sung by every child on the street. It didn't take Billy much to start talking. One thing Khumbo had already established about his brother; he didn't need much drink to be loquacious.

He looked tidier today, with his beard combed and hair patted low. He had left his jacket at the office, but his necktie was well in place. As he caressed his beard his gigantic body never ceased to tower over the other two, like a combatant whose victory over his rival had already been decided by *Mulengi*, the creator. Sam remained subdued throughout, rather cagey about getting too involved in any subject. If Billy's outburst yesterday was any indication of what he had to put .up with, very few would blame him for opting for a passive role.

'I don't know what you were expecting,' Billy started rather boisterously. 'But here you don't just arrive today and start work tomorrow. Sam, tell him.'

Sam nodded and sipped his beer.

'You have to get stripped of your westernism,' went on Billy. 'You agree with me, Sam?'

Sam took another sip. Then he belched: 'Well, yes and no. That used to be the case in the seventies, not any more. Now it's just a question of inefficiency.'

'But why would anyone want to do that?' Khumbo's intervention turned out to be the very encouragement Billy was soliciting.

'Why? Did you say why?' His eyes were blazing again. 'I'll tell you why.' He loosened his necktie as his forehead moistened.

Sam concentrated on his drink, still finding the situation disconcerting. Khumbo ordered another round of drinks which he hoped would be the last, since their dishes had by now been cleared away. Already Billy had had more than enough. But this discussion was becoming interesting, as evidenced by the furrows on Khumbo's face. In moments of concentration his forehead was always invaded by deep furrows.

'Listen,' Billy continued. 'You smell western and that smell must go. That's why. It's a whole acculturation process – that's what my sociology lecturer would have said.' He stood up. 'Nature calls,' he announced as he headed for the toilet.

'I must say he sounds pretty reckless,' Khumbo suggested as a way of dragging Sam into the conversation, but deep down not caring about the statement either way.

'Everyone in town fears for him. He'll say what he likes anywhere. There are times I don't feel safe with him. He has these weird contacts with some South African drivers. And that is dangerous.'

'What contacts?'

But before Sam could answer, Billy staggered in.

He sat down and announced that under the circumstances he considered it imprudent to return to the office. Khumbo let the South African subject drop for a moment. He would pursue it later.

'Sam, my dear friend,' he pleaded. 'Kindly report my

indisposition.' And then as an afterthought, 'Only when asked.'

With that they left, passing the offices where Sam staggered out, leaving Billy and Khumbo beside themselves with laughter.

'Follow my example and go home to sleep it off,' Billy shouted to him.

Sam obeyed and staggered back into the car.

The two brothers spent most of the afternoon making up for staying up late last night. Khumbo was the first to stir in bed and after rubbing his eyes hard, he responded to the urge to relieve his bladder. Upon his return, all he could do was reflect on the situation he had walked into. Billy didn't seem the same innocent boy he had left behind. In spite of the strong evidence of cohabitation in the house, which included Sam's question yesterday, Billy himself behaved single and never mentioned any lady's name. He had become secretive on personal matters and quite verbose on others. He obviously had strong views on the establishment.

Then he thought of writing Sue, but gave up on realising that he had to wait for Billy to wake up and provide him with a writing pad or buy one himself tomorrow, although he didn't have much to say to her yet. 'Tea or coffee?' It was Billy who gave him a start, filling the doorway to his room with his volume, definitely looking better than at lunch time.

'Tea, please,' he jumped out of bed to display his sprightly nature.

Khumbo had always had time for sport. In school it had been soccer, making himself a hero among the girls and young boys with his dribbling and frequent and often effortless scoring. In England he had had no time for soccer. In fact it had taken him close to two years before he could participate in any sport. First, it was tennis and then, later on, by sheer chance somebody offered to teach him squash. The latter turned out most convenient in terms of actual time spent on the court and the intensity of the exercise offered by the game. He had never looked back. As a result his drinking had been well under control, usually confined to the hour or two immediately following his game when he felt totally dehydrated and required gallons of liquid to restore his body to its balanced self. He quietly hoped his new company at home wouldn't lead him into substituting drinking for his squash.

Billy offered him tea in a cup on a saucer which was strange after all the casual years of mugs. He carried his cup and walked to the window and drank from it standing, as if to assure himself that the fitness had not yet disappeared.

'Where is your wife, *ada*?' he found himself asking.

Billy put his cup down on the stool, and then clasped his hands. Khumbo cracked and locked his knuckles while biting his lower lip. The furrows were back on his forehead. Khumbo watched Billy studiously, this time intent on getting some answers to some of the serious questions he had. His clean-shaven face contrasted sharply with Billy's, just as did his relatively small body against his brother's.

Billy's beard quivered for some time before he uttered anything. Khumbo wondered whether it was just the drinking that affected his brother's deportment.

Billy sipped his tea twice and decided it was cool enough to be drained at one go. He put the cup down slowly.

'I'm married. But father will not bless my marriage. I haven't quarrelled with him, but neither have I given up my choice. I sent her home to mother because she is expecting our baby. Any time now.'

He only continued on realising that Khumbo wouldn't say anything at that point, although his face said it all, incredulous and dissatisfied.

'Go home for a week or two. See them and then come back. You might ask more relevant questions then.' He poured himself another cup of tea. Khumbo offered his for a refill. They drank in silence.

'Do you have a writing pad?' Khumbo asked, for the sheer desire to return the atmosphere to normal.

'No. But we can drive downtown. The supermarket will still be open.'

And so they drove downtown. Still the atmosphere did not return to normal.

* * *

The shopping centre was full and busy, now that it was after working hours. Cars were parked everywhere and people rushed around waving hello to this one and goodbye to that one. Billy was no exception. Then somebody called Billy's name.

'Excuse me, *ada*,' Billy said. 'I've got to see somebody. You'll find me at the car.'

'Fine,' Khumbo said, as he disappeared into the arcade in search of the supermarket.

When he came out, Billy was just jumping out of one of the three trucks that had parked on the main road. A man jumped out too, in yellow overalls and wearing a cap. He too was a big fellow. Another man in similar attire remained at the wheel and waved goodbye to Billy. The one on the ground shook Billy's hand vigorously. Billy walked back to the car and handed the car keys to Khumbo. They entered the car and drove back in silence. Driving past the trucks, Khumbo noticed their foreign registration.

'I think you shouldn't go until I've had the car serviced.' Billy suggested.

'Well, well…' Khumbo stammered in embarrassment. 'I should be the one to pay for that, but it'll take a while before my money is transferred.'

'I can manage,' Billy said. 'You needn't worry.'

'Thank you,' Khumbo said and left it at that.

Khumbo was disturbed late that night by some noises in the sitting-room, all of them male voices. Three or four.

He was too tired to get the details of the conversation. And so he fell asleep again.

In the morning he noticed that all the curios that had decorated the sitting-room (he had counted five wooden carvings) had gone.

'What happened to the carvings?' he asked.

'I sold them,' Billy answered unperturbed.

'When?'

'Last night.'

'Who to?'

'Does it matter?'

'Of course it matters. 'Cause I would have bought them if I had known they were for sale.' Khumbo explained.

'You wouldn't have,' Billy continued casually. 'Far too expensive.'

'Is that how you can service the car?' Khumbo sneered.

'Yes, my brother.' Billy answered with a rare smile on his face. 'That's how. That and much more.'

A quick tremor ran down Khumbo's spine but he chose not to ask further questions until he and Sam had talked.

Chapter Two

It took several days to have the car serviced. A mechanic had to be found privately and a price agreed before the expert could work on the car and before Khumbo could get started for Nkhotakota. Days later, Khumbo sat in the bar at Capital Hotel. He didn't feel like starting off at seven-thirty in the morning since it was only a two-hour drive, that is if the car behaved itself. So, after driving Billy to work he returned to the hotel bar. The bar wasn't the same without the hubbub of the night when drinkers gossiped, jeered and even compared notes on women. There was a tacit agreement among drinkers, at least according to his experience so far, that women constituted the main agenda during these informal meetings. Other items – economics or politics, etc. – did not, by the same token, seem to play a part in their lives. Except, of course, where somebody like Billy chose to operate outside the norms. Khumbo carried his glass outside into the shade by the fish pond. The loneliness here was compensated for by the twittering birds perching on the reeds and shrubs in the pond. The creepers forming the shade above him took care of the glare from the fierce sun.

He started a lively letter to Sue, filling in all the details from the airport down to the interview (if one could describe such a farce as an interview) at the Training Office. But half-way through the narration he abandoned the epistle in favour of a post card, on which he simply reported safe arrival and promised to write later when he had settled down.

At about ten o'clock he left for Nkhotakota after having the car checked again for oil. An extra pint and a full tank concluded the preparations. It took him twenty minutes to leave the city and start enjoying the countryside. The volume of traffic on the Lilongwe-Salima road had increased tremendously, and so had the volume of roadside trade – pancakes, jam sandwiches, sugarcane, papaya, etc. But then these market spots would be interrupted by stretches of grassland and wild forests, rivers and mountains, the latter resulting in steep slopes which inflicted unwelcome punishment on the car. Twice he had to stop due to overheating, the second time close to a small market so that he spent his time chewing a sugarcane he bought. The pleasure created by swallowing the sweet juice threw him into reminiscences of a childhood in which eating sugarcane had formed the core of social activities – playing in their various age groups, meeting with elders, particularly grannies, as they fulfilled their social functions with folklore and narrations of events of the past including the Arab slave trade and the white missionaries. They had spent few holidays with their grandparents.

The sweet juice took him back to Gogo, years back. The old man had insisted on having his grandchildren spend their Christmas holiday with him. He himself did not believe in Christmas, but he made sure he grabbed any opportunity that presented itself by way of a holiday to coax Baba into releasing the children. Baba's concession to such demands took the form of Khumbo and Billy. The girls were always too small to accompany the boys.

They started off for the village on a bus that travelled on that route only once a day. If you missed it you either walked the 22 miles or waited for the morrow. It meant arriving at the bus stage at least an hour before the expected time. Waving goodbye was the best part of it all. They approached their bus stop, clad in dust delivered by courtesy of the ever-disintegrating metal box they called bus. It had spent the last one-and-a-half hours rattling on the dirt road, stopping every 500 yards, dropping off or picking up a lone passenger here and there, or for the crew to quench their thirst with some *masese* brew. These brief stops were a temptation to everyone with a pocket which could accommodate more than a bus ticket. So with the driver went a few others. In the end it was just the driver, conductor and one passenger, who called himself Duli.

Now, Duli was the name of the Zimbabwean boxer who became a hero of some international repute by defeating several South African and Zambian boxers. Up to now

Khumbo had not been able to establish whether the man on the bus was actually the Duli he had heard so much about, but for the moment it sufficed to hear someone talking real boxing stuff. He and Billy had talked about that bus trip for a long time afterwards.

'*Manje*, I miss boxing,' Duli said as he came up the bus steps, belching out some foul *masese* breath. *Manje* was the only Shona word that kept coming up to justify his been-to story.

'*Manje*, I can't forget Gwanzura stadium. My, that was a fight with Jeketuli. He came at me like a hornless bull, charging but nothing else.'

Then he would demonstrate the jabs as he steadied himself by leaning against a seat, oblivious of the shake and rattle that kept shoving and swaying the passengers.

'I brought about Jeketuli's downfall,' he laughed so loud the driver had to look behind. Jeketuli had been another of those legendary names at the time. 'I was the talk of Gwanzura. The Nyasa boy, that's it. That's what they would say. And I would shout back "Duli!!!" Oh, Gwanzura. I miss Gwanzura.'

Next stop he got out as the *kanyenya* boys stormed the bus, one selling boiled and curried eggs, another fried chicken pieces, and yet another *utaka*.

'I'll have *kanyenya*,' Billy said, stretching his hand for money.

'Baba said we shouldn't spend the money on the bus,' Khumbo replied.

'I want my money. I am hungry.'

'Billy!' Khumbo said under his breath to avoid a scene.

'I'll have a chicken,' Billy declared and dipped his hand into Khumbo's pocket. Khumbo knew enough trouble signals from Billy.

'Okay, wait then.'

Khumbo stood up to look for the *kanyenya* boy.

'How much is the chicken?'

'Leg one Kwacha, Wing 50 tambala. Breast two Kwacha. Neck…'

'Give me two legs.'

He gave the boy the two Kwacha and received his two pieces on a piece of dirty old newspaper. The amount of chilli on the chicken took Billy by surprise. But he endured the test, preferring to cough and sneeze rather than give it up.

By the time the crew returned, it was difficult to tell which *kanyenya* smell dominated on the bus – the fish or chicken or the eggs or goat meat. There was more coughing than chattering. At least half the bus could afford the favourite snack. The rough ride was more bearable after that.

The two boys would join Gogo in laughter and the rest of the crowd which had come with him would follow spontaneously. The whole village came to welcome the town boys, admire their smooth faces and clean clothes, and share whatever gifts they had brought to the old man. As they approached the cluster of thatched houses,

Khumbo's preoccupation was a sugarcane – how he would tear through the skin to the juicy stick inside and let his mouth water and drip with the sweet juice as his teeth crushed the cane into chaff.

'So, who is going to the woods with the goats tomorrow?' Gogo's question came with his usual chuckle, teasingly.

The boys hesitated as they exchanged glances.

'Scared, hey?' Gogo teased further and the other members of the party laughed with him.

Khumbo and Billy just walked on silently, unwilling to forget their experience two years ago when the town boys had been put in their place by the village herdboys.

The fight had been arranged by Bomba, the oldest of the herdboys, as a way of confirming the existing lines of authority. If Khumbo beat his opponent then he would take over as second in command, which would have meant having a lieutenant to look after Gogo's goats and sharing the morning's collections (usually food items).

Khumbo lost to bony Majiga and in his frustration left the goats behind as he and Billy returned home to report the incident. They had never gone back to the woods after that.

Now all Khumbo wanted to hear of was sugarcane. That was his idea of a holiday.

'I don't see any sugarcane selling anywhere,' Khumbo remarked in order to change the subject to something more palatable.

'No sugarcane, sorry,' Gogo chuckled.

'Why?' Billy asked, disappointed.

'It's rainy season. The cane is still growing. It's very salty – you wouldn't like it. Come again in April.'

For the first time Khumbo saw the relationship between seasons and sugarcane. Suddenly, the trip became purposeless – the roundness of the thatched house became antiquated and uncivilised. He wanted to go back home and spend his Christmas with Mai Nabanda and Baba and Paweme and Ellen. The teasing from the old man soured the atmosphere even more.

'Ohhh, I know my young man here,' announced Gogo as soon as they sat down on the *khonde* of his big hut. His was the biggest, and he had the biggest *makola* of goats and cattle. 'He won't forgive me until he has chewed some cane. Hey, Rajab, go behind and bring me two sugarcanes. We'll break the rules for our honoured guests.' Rajab scampered away, knowing what was in it for him too.

Khumbo couldn't resist a smile. Billy laughed openly. The chickens cackled and danced beautifully, and the dung smell suddenly fell into place. Gogo's laughter and the laughter of those who had joined him to make this a joyous occasion had now acquired a rhythm which was harmonious with the goats and chickens and cattle and sugarcane. Khumbo's mind raced ahead – when the house flooded with *nsima* and chicken dishes from all over, he would eat it all up to his tummy's satisfaction. Every villager would bring a chicken dish or an egg dish – just for him and Billy. He and his brother would make sure they emptied every one of them.

'Here you are,' Gogo announced, interrupting his wishful thinking.

They grabbed a sugarcane each and tore into it.

It was softer than usual. For the moment it didn't matter. They sat on the *khonde*, watched by the curious villagers, and went through the first piece. By the time they came to the second, something was really wrong with the delicacy.

'Can I have a bit of yours?' Billy asked Khumbo.

'Why?' Khumbo pretended not to know the reason.

'Mine is salty,' Billy said, throwing it away.

'Mine too,' Khumbo muttered inaudibly.

They heard Gogo's big laugh even before they had thrown the sugarcane away. At that point Billy did miss his grandmother, who had passed away two years before.

'As we say here in the village, it is only after he has broken a tooth eating a bone that a child will know why his mother always gave him meat.'

Billy and Khumbo withdrew to the other side of the *nkhokwe* to reflect on their misery and dim prospects for the next two weeks: maybe he'd let them swim in the lake… maybe there would be *nthudza* in the bush… maybe *masuku*…

'Ya, *mdala*. *Nkhuku* for K2.50.' A man carrying an unwilling cockerel tapped him on the shoulder.

'Not interested,' replied Khumbo.

'Two Kwacha. That's cheap.'

'I don't want it,' insisted Khumbo as he looked away.

'Last price: K1.50.'

There was no response from Khumbo.

'Hey, *mdala*, you can spare a poor man K1.50. Ya?' Khumbo turned round.

'I am not buying it, and that's that.'

'Big man like you? Want us to go stealing?' He moved closer to Khumbo with the bird cackling away. Khumbo moved further down to the grocery, but the man pressed on.

'Want me to steal, ya?'

Khumbo had just thrown away the last piece of sugarcane, having lost interest in it on account of a stranger with a cockerel which he wasn't interested in, even if it was offered to him free, when he saw a mob of angry villagers coming round the grocery. One pointed at the scene which he had now become part of. Then they surged towards him.

Khumbo was so lost he didn't notice the stranger fleeing and the cockerel disappearing into the bush. It was only after the mob had rushed past him that he recovered his composure enough to enjoy the drama. Three boys chased the cockerel while the rest went after the man amidst shouts of 'Thief… stop thief…!'

He managed a smile and returned to the car. He opened the bonnet and unscrewed the radiator cap. The car needed more water. He approached the men on the grocery verandah.

'Excuse me,' he started, addressing nobody in particular, 'Where can I find water?'

The tailor continued with his sewing, the shoemaker with his shoes, and the tinsmith rearranging his pots.

'Excuse me, I need help,' pleaded Khumbo.

'He needs help,' said the tailor looking at the shoemaker.

'Well, give it to him, then,' advised the shoemaker.

'Hm,' the tinsmith grunted. 'Help indeed! Has he just seen us?'

'Young man,' the tailor called. 'Whose hand have you shaken?'

'I am sure he has even forgotten how to shake hands,' the tinsmith concluded.

The three burst into laughter and continued in their respective engagements, leaving him rooted to the ground in total stupidity, musing over the accuracy of the comments as if they knew he had been away for a long time. To the three men, anyone who didn't know how to address his elders was simply a spoilt town boy who had thrown his good manners to the wind in search of a life he didn't even understand. Khumbo dragged his feet towards the car, slammed the bonnet closed, started it, and drove off to loud laughter from the verandah. On his left the cockerel was flapping and cackling in the hands of one of his captors. On the right, as he engaged fourth gear, he had a glimpse of the stranger trying to free himself from his captors, helpless against the shower of blows landing freely on his defenceless head and body.

Khumbo was annoyed with himself for behaving in the manner he had done, especially for leaving the place more annoyed than apologetic. When he looked at the speedometer it still read 0 m.p.h. Then he remembered that very few things worked in this car and reduced speed accordingly. He stopped at the next river and topped up the radiator before continuing on the journey.

As he drove into the little town of Nkhotakota the juxtaposition of mosques and churches bore evidence of the ongoing battle between the followers of the symbols. The social divisions were only buried by the children whose free mixing must have been the cause of much heartache among adults. But such was the power of hypocrisy that Moslems and Christians alike dared not rebuke their children on the playground. By the same token, the little ones took full advantage of their parents' impotence in public and conducted their experiments in cultural cross-fertilisation in broad daylight. What went on in their little homes under the cover of darkness was not allowed to interfere with the glory of the song, dance and ululation under the cover of the sun. They chewed sugarcane together, and went swimming and fishing in the shallow waters of the big lake together.

The lake was the source of fish and life. Boys learnt to swim in it long before they could fish. But, in the end, a boy could hardly wait for the big smile on his mother's face as her son dangled a *chambo* or *ncheni* on a straw and improved the meal prospects of the day. Mothers would then exchange notes on how well their sons were doing on their way to manhood and subsistence. As they grew older their skills would include paddling canoes into waters further up or down the lake.

He was amazed by the little town's resistance to change. All along he had been alarmed by the newness of things – even people's attitudes. The very road that took him from Salima to Nkhotakota was a continuation of an all-season lakeshore highway started and completed in his absence. It continued to Dwangwa while he turned into the narrower, sand-laden and unchanging road.

He was thrown back once again to his childhood. The mango tree and the sugarcane bushes were still as he had left them. The yellow flowers were still struggling against the otherwise all-conquering sun, thanks to persistent watering. The bougainvillaea had crept on to the roof, making it the only item to defy the unchanging scene around it.

Nkhotakota had benefited culturally from the Arab slave trade in that architecturally it belonged to the orient. The star and moon were a familiar sight, just as the mosque was. Originally anyone who was seen at the one-time church school was considered a traitor by the largely Moslem community. This had always made Khumbo wonder how it would be received if he decided to marry Chimwemwe. But that was only a hypothetical problem now as he hadn't heard from her for years. Her letters had just fizzled out. Chimwemwe was one of the few girls whose presence at the school had been a direct result of the government's efforts to persuade Moslems to send their children to school, now that they didn't have to abandon their religion for the sake of education, as in the colonial days.

He knocked on the only door he knew.

'So we have a visitor!' he heard a voice from behind.

When he turned round, it was to examine the physical details of the speaker rather than identify him.

'Baba!' he cried and rushed back to the street to shake his hand.

'My son,' he said as he held out his right hand, leaving the left to follow and cover the upper side of Khumbo's hand.

For a whole minute they just looked at each other, each face telling a story, each bosom full to bursting point with questions that were best unasked, unanswered. Baba's hair had gone grey; one had to look hard for black strands; but it was still parted in the middle. He was using spectacles. The face, once well padded, now had a number of projections, exposing the sharpness of certain features.

'Eight years!' sighed Baba, releasing Khumbo's hand.

'Eight years,' Khumbo agreed.

'Eight long years,' Baba repeated. 'I thought they would never end. Let's go inside and see for yourself how empty it is now.'

They climbed the two steps leading to the verandah and Baba fished a bunch of keys from his pocket. He opened the door and allowed Khumbo to enter first. Khumbo proceeded towards the door at the opposite end of the room which led to the kitchen. After unlocking it, he was surprised to see that there was a man cooking in the kitchen. The man turned round, saw Khumbo and nearly fainted. It was the same old Kachala.

'*Bwana!*' Kachala almost screamed.

'*Kachala!*' Khumbo said, accepting this pleasant surprise more for his father's sake than his own.

The two exchanged a few compliments on each other's good looks and health and then Khumbo went back inside. His father had been watching him all along, basking in the glory of Khumbo's achievements. Dr Khumbo Dala! When Khumbo returned he surveyed the sitting-room, as he cracked his knuckles, noting the details which could have led to his father's remarks about its emptiness. Most of the chairs were missing, the only imposing furniture being the dining set. Four armchairs were placed around a rectangular coffee table and it was here that both retired; but not before studying the pictures in a frame on the wall. It was only after he had sat down that Khumbo noticed the tall, new stand on which rested a paraffin lamp which, as he discovered later, was put to more use than the erratic electric lights.

They sat to lunch which Kachala proudly served. He went about his chores with renewed vigour, as if Khumbo's arrival had given him a new lease of life. Baba also noticed this change in a man who never gave in to emotions.

When it came to saying grace, Baba used the same old phrases, the same gestures and the same guttural tone. As in the old days, his pace dropped to half its normal rate as if to ensure polite and accurate transmission. He offered special thanks for the safe arrival of 'one who lived among strangers in a far land'.

'I hope you will enjoy the fish,' remarked Baba when they started eating. 'You came so unannounced we couldn't offer a chicken at such short notice.'

'I'll be fine,' he assured Baba, and went on to enjoy the *chambo* which he hadn't had for as long as he had been away.

He didn't have time to remember how a *chambo* tasted if prepared by female hands. In fact, given the choice, he would have preferred the fish to chicken in the evening, tomorrow, day after tomorrow... But that could never be; the only traditional welcome a valued guest can receive is the one expressed through the chicken meal.

'It's nice you're back,' Baba said, unable to take his eyes off Khumbo, amused by the hands removing bones from meat with the same old dexterity.

'I couldn't wait to get back.'

'It's really nice,' Baba repeated as he poured more fish gravy on to Khumbo's plate. For the *nsima* and fish to glide down your throat, you had to dip your lump into as much gravy as possible.

The absence of vegetables, *nkhwani* or *mpiru* reminded Khumbo of the problems faced by the little town in the dry season.

'I miss *nkhwani*,' he remarked instinctively.

'I wish I had known of your coming. Kachala would have gone looking for vegetables.'

'Not to worry,' Khumbo said to correct what might have been a wrong impression created by his seeming dissatisfaction with his father's warm reception.

Baba's smile revealed a new face to his son. It pulled at the skin around the jaw and down the neck. This made Khumbo wonder whether the shirts he had brought would not hang loosely around the neck and shoulders which once had boasted sinews and not veins.

'I have to go back to work,' Baba announced, interrupting what had been a truly enjoyable meal. He picked up his walking stick. Years ago it would have served a punitive purpose as well.

'I will walk you down to the office,' Khumbo offered.

'Not necessary,' protested the father. 'I'll just hop along.'

'I need the walk,' Khumbo insisted as he left the table to wash his hands, unwilling to let go this precious opportunity to be by his father's side again.

Baba disappeared into the kitchen to issue instructions for supper, which chicken to slaughter, and what should go with it. He locked the door and they walked out into the street.

'Is the car safe where it is?' Khumbo asked as they walked past it.

'For the time being, yes,' Baba replied. 'In the evening we will have to park it behind the house, next to the bedroom window. Just to be on the safe side. But,' he added as an afterthought, 'we better take the luggage inside now.'

So they returned to the car and removed the suitcase and the other smaller items – magazines, newspapers, novels, etc. – and took them back to the house.

After walking him to the office – that is after answering numerous greetings called out from almost every verandah of the houses lining the street to the office – Khumbo took a walk around the old town. The eyes followed him wherever he went as if he were a mobile curio.

Jussab's shop was now run by a Malawian. Not successfully, he thought. Most Asians had, since independence, confined their operations to the cities and big towns only. The smell of fish hit him as he approached the market. Fish has a pleasant smell only when cooked, not before. He walked past the market deaf to the pleas from the sellers for him to buy this cassava or that flour or even love potions.

The urge to see his old school welled up inside him. He took the main road which took him round to the shopping centre and market. By the time he got to the school so many memories of about fifteen years back had flooded into his mind. The school was now in two blocks: the first being the old dilapidated brick building and the second, new and better looking. He stopped to watch a class on the football ground engaged in physical education. In spite of the futile nature of the engagement in terms of future use, he caught himself nursing some nostalgia about his own participation many years earlier. Funny that he could not recall a single name he could associate the ground with. At least he was content that the sight was familiar.

A hand tapped him on the shoulder. He turned round.

'Pempho!' he exclaimed.

'Khumbo!' answered the other. 'I mean Doctor!'

They shook hands vigorously.

'Drop the doctor business,' Khumbo demanded. 'How are you?'

'Me? All right, I guess,' Pempho answered, still holding the other's hand. 'How are you?'

'I am fine – and really glad to see you again after so long,' Khumbo replied. 'In fact,' he continued, 'I was just trying to remember at least one face from fifteen years ago.'

'Fifteen years!' sighed Pempho. 'It sounds a lifetime.'

'It sounds so short to me,' corrected Khumbo.

'Depends what you have been doing,' Pempho continued in a negative vein. Khumbo felt a little guilty.

'Come,' Pempho said. 'I'll show you around your old school. And then I'll introduce you to my staff and pupils.'

'My staff and...' Khumbo stammered. 'You don't mean...'

'Yes, that's what I mean.' Pempho cut him short,

smiling. 'Some of us developed such affinity for the old place we just can't get away from it.'

'How interesting!' That was all Khumbo could manage in return, deep down feeling uncomfortable about the gap between them that could never be bridged.

As they walked towards the school, Khumbo felt genuinely sorry for Pempho. To be trapped inside those walls as a child, have a bit of freedom spending the next six years away from the place, and end up within the confines of the same walls, was a predicament he was glad to have escaped.

They entered the headmaster's office.

'This is my office now,' Pempho announced.

'The same old office,' Khumbo commented. 'Nothing has changed, then.'

'There has been change, Khumbo,' Pempho said as he offered his guest a chair. 'We have more Moslem children, the parents' meetings are getting more and more stormy, mostly since we have to accommodate religious differences. There is the expansion to the buildings. The teachers, for example, are getting younger and more disillusioned with the profession, the low salaries plus the low status. Any chance to get into a different job, in the city particularly, is most welcome. But those openings are almost non-existent these days. So everybody feels trapped in this little town, the only outlet being in bars, and the social consequences of that option are obvious.'

Khumbo listened to his friend, and all he could offer was sympathy which he dared not express in words, knowing that opening his mouth by way of comment or question would lead to another misunderstood utterance. The desk was orderly but full of text books and exercise books. A timetable hung on the wall opposite Pempho's desk. The only other hanging was a calendar.

'Let me show you the classroom,' Pempho offered.

'Well, that's not necessary,' said Khumbo.

'You don't know what inspiration you can be to some of those desperate children.' Pempho paused, but continued only after seeing that Khumbo's reply was not forthcoming. 'Can I ask you to meet my pupils, please? We do it with a lot of visitors. But you will be the first Doctor, and just arrived from overseas at that. Can you imagine what you will be doing to those kids?'

'Listen,' Khumbo said firmly. 'I am not prepared to parade through half a dozen classrooms pretending I am black Moses.'

'Okay, how many classrooms, then?' Pempho insisted.

'None.'

Pempho looked at Khumbo and thought a while before saying anything further.

'I can't understand you. Just now you told me fifteen years was a short time. How, then, can you have forgotten yourself sitting on one of those hard benches – sometimes on the floor – being told that if you want to be like Dr or Mr so and so you must work hard. You must listen to what

I am saying. You must do your homework! Those children have dreams. But right now their dreams are not about London or New York, but those of leaving this school for a good secondary school, in the city if possible. You can inspire some towards that goal. But here you are, standing aloof…'

'I am not standing aloof,' protested Khumbo.

'What do you think you are doing, then?'

Pempho's question was interrupted by a knock and then a lady entered.

'Can I have some chalk, sir?' she enquired of Pempho. The 'sir' betrayed her lisp.

'Miss Ndele, you know I only issue chalk once a week. And rules are rules; if you don't find your rations adequate, then you have to buy your own extra.'

'But sir, you know my class can be unruly,' she pleaded. 'When I came back after break the chalk was missing from the box.'

'Find the culprits and punish them.'

'I have tried that before and you know they won't take a woman seriously. Can you come and talk to them yourself?'

He looked at her severely and then melted.

'This once only,' he said as he counted five more pieces of chalk. 'Next time don't count on me or my sympathy.'

As Pempho counted the pieces of chalk, Miss Ndele stole a glance at Khumbo and through a sideways look managed to memorise a few details about him. Much to her relief, the headmaster spoke as she was about to leave.

'By the way,' he said, 'Meet my visitor, Dr Dala. Khumbo, this charming young lady here is our standard 8 teacher, Miss Ndele.'

'How do you do, sir?' Miss Ndele lisped as she shook his hand.

Khumbo mumbled something as he concentrated on the smile and handshake. The lisping was becoming something of an attraction, as if it was the bait with which she hooked her victims.

'So what are you doing tonight, madam?' Pempho asked. Her eyes dropped in slight embarrassment. 'I thought you might want to come over this evening so you can ask all the questions about England. Dr Dala has just arrived from England, you know.'

'No, I can't,' intercepted Khumbo. 'I just promised Baba I'll be home this evening. We have some family problems to discuss.'

'Tomorrow, then,' Pempho pursued relentlessly.

'Tomorrow is fine by me,' agreed Miss Ndele before Khumbo could ruin the rare prospect.

Khumbo nodded his head in total amusement.

'And Dr Dala has also agreed to speak to the school assembly tomorrow.' Pempho gambled with his friend's temper, hoping that the lady's presence would work miracles.

It did.

'That's very nice of him,' Miss Ndele said. 'Thank you so much, sir,' she added, turning to Khumbo.

Khumbo found himself swayed by the composure and charm of the young lady which stood almost incongruously to the unchanging town which still had nothing to boast but age and obstinacy. Somehow he was drawn to her intrinsic aggressiveness and independence which he found refreshing.

She wasn't tall; neither was she short. The weight was distributed evenly about her, allowing the yellow knitted blouse to do justice to her curves before disappearing into the deep green pleated skirt. The difference with her counterparts in the city was the naturalness in her hair and on her face as evidenced by the maintenance of natural curl in the case of the former and the absence of colour on her lips in the case of the latter.

His friend, on the other hand, amazed him in the way he seemed to accept things as they had been, the result of which was the aged appearance of his face, body and clothes. He did not seem to do anything about his weight, whose graph had already comfortably lodged in the obesity zone. He wasn't a tall man which, in all fairness, explained the unseemly appearance.

Back in Lilongwe Billy examined his new car, a VW Golf, cream, and with a South African registration. Inside he was impressed but he had learnt not to show his feelings, especially when driving bargains. He looked at his South African counterparts and attempted a smile, a hint that he had accepted this part of the deal.

'Where is the money?' Billy moved on to the next part of the deal, looking Rex straight in the eye.

'Well,' Rex started, 'there's a bit of a problem there…'

'What problem?' Billy didn't even let him finish.

'Well, the boss, he says the goods were second grade,' Rex said calmly.

'Since when has he found fault with my goods?' Billy was now showing signs of agitation.

'We really couldn't, I mean can't ask him that…' Rex ventured.

'You couldn't, eh?' Billy pulled his beard as he went round the car, in an effort to calm himself.

Rex said something to his fellow truck driver. Billy didn't hear it and therefore let it go in spite of his mounting fury.

'How much did you declare it for?' Billy asked finally, seemingly calmer.

'K15,000,' Rex answered.

'And you know how much duty I'll have to pay?'

'Ken has the exact figure,' Rex said, prompting his friend to show Billy the receipt.

'Ten thousand and six-two Kwacha,' Ken, the more timid of the two truck drivers, said as he presented Billy with the documents. Ken did not look Billy in the eyes.

Billy let go his beard and stood arms akimbo as ideas

raced wildly through his mind, struggling with the temptation to lock his large hands around their necks one by one. They had won this round, another round. He would have his one of these days.

The three of them now got into the Golf, Billy behind the wheel for a proper test drive as he took them to the city centre to their truck.

'How much have you got this time?' Rex asked.

'Not much,' Billy answered excitedly, momentarily being caught off guard. He would need the money to pay the car duty.

'But enough to make the boss smile.'

'In that case let's get it first and then drop us off after,' Rex suggested. Billy obliged.

By the time Billy had parted company with Rex and Ken that night, he was the happiest drunken man on earth. Not only could he do away with the old wreck of the Renault 16, he could now look his wife in the face and afford to meet her demands. He hadn't done badly lately. The truck was doing fine on a government contract supplying vegetables to schools in Lilongwe. Now he could afford a more comfortable car. Not a Mercedes, but more comfortable than the Renault. His mother was a star. What would he have done without her? Chimwemwe would soon be the happiest woman in Malawi. His ambition was to open a shop for her.

By the time Billy had parked his Golf and staggered towards his door, it was well after midnight. He went straight to the toilet and relieved his bladder noisily while part-humming and part-singing *shauliyako*, the East African rumba version. He then walked straight into the kitchen, oblivious to Sam's entry through the half-shut door. He attempted whistling, which ended in dismal failure. Then he heard the coughing.

'Who is there?' he shouted in his drunken slur.

'Sam!'

'What now? It's late,' asked Billy still in the kitchen, fetching a frying pan. He could only manage an egg judging by the contents of the fridge.

'Trouble,' Sam said candidly.

'I don't mind trouble,' Billy said, now staggering into the sitting-room, a frying pan in one hand, an egg in the other. 'I've always been in trouble. See Sam, my name should have been Trouble or *Mabvuto*.'

'Sit down, Billy,' Sam said, 'This is big trouble.'

'Then I should have been big trouble,' Billy said.

'Can I have a beer?' Sam's nerves were letting him down again. They always did when Billy was drunk.

'Help yourself.'

'The police were here,' Sam said as he went to the kitchen to get himself a beer.

Billy suddenly became quiet.

'Where have you been since you left the office?' Sam queried.

'Drinking, alone,' Billy found himself saying, rather inaudibly.

'Well,' Sam said, 'You can hide it from me, but they know it all. The car, the truck drivers, the curios.' For some reason Sam found himself saying it all, without stammering.

'What curios?' Billy was now standing steady.

'Billy, this is real trouble. Better start looking for help – a lawyer maybe.'

'What are you talking about?' Billy's slur was now clearing.

'If you have nothing to hide, fine,' Sam said. 'But they took away those curios under the bed.'

'The bastards!' Billy said as he jumped up and shot into the bedroom.

He switched on the light and took in everything at a glance. His mattress was on the floor, torn open, and his suitcases were gaping at him as well. Through the springs he could see the floor under the bed. All the carvings had gone.

He came out and went straight into Khumbo's room, shoving aside Sam who had followed him to stand in the doorway. Khumbo's cases had been forced open and every single item had been thrown out. Some cases would never lock again, others could but what use would they be with knife cuts half a metre long? 'Someone will pay for this,' he mumbled to himself, grinding his teeth.

'There wasn't anything I could do,' Sam apologised.

'Uniformed or plain clothes?' Billy asked.

'Plain.'

'How many?'

'Four.'

Billy's eyes were suddenly ablaze.

'Oh, Sam,' Billy ground his teeth, holding Sam by the collar with both hands.

'Billy!' Sam cried, 'You are hurting me!'

'Can't you see, Sam? Couldn't you see?' he said, still holding on to the collar. 'Thieves, that's what they are!'

'But how was I supposed to know…' Sam pleaded.

'How? The numbers,' Billy explained impatiently. 'Police don't come in fours. One or two. Never in a gang.'

'But they didn't steal anything.'

'What about my curios?' Billy now let go of the collar.

Billy went back to the door and then realised that he didn't remember opening it. He examined the lock. A careful job, no mess. They had deliberately left it open. He now staggered back into the room, threw himself into a chair and relapsed into his drunken stupor. Sam just looked on.

'Do you know how much each of these curios is worth?' Billy asked.

Sam shook his head.

'You are better off not knowing, anyway,' Billy concluded as he stood up. He took the egg and frying pan back to the kitchen.

'Tell me exactly what happened,' Billy enquired.

'I was in the sitting room listening to BBC "Focus on Africa" when I saw the lights come on. So I came to see who it was as I had heard a car stop just before them. You had no car, you see. And it wasn't the truck.'

'Did you say a car?'

'Yes, why?'

'Not ordinary thieves, then?'

'I wouldn't say so, Billy. It was a police car.'

Billy's palms moistened.

'How do you know?'

'It was Cortina with a ZA registration.'

'Hm, that sounds like police all right.'

'Apart from the truck, do you have another car I don't know about?'

'Yes.'

'A Golf?'

'Yes.'

'When did you get it?'

'Well…' Billy was at a loss. 'Why all these questions?'

'Because I want to know if I lied,' Sam answered.

'Did you?'

'Yes!' Sam said emphatically. 'I said you had no other small cars. And here you are driving a brand new Golf.'

'I just bought it.'

'Yes, I know that, thanks to the police.'

Billy rose to go to the bedroom.

'Goodnight, Sam,' he said as he disappeared into his room. 'Close the door for me as you go out. You are behaving like a policeman yourself.'

Sam hesitated before the next question, not even sure if he should ask it at all. But he must…

'Billy, do you have a farm?'

Billy froze in his stride. Nobody, not even his most trusted customer, knew about his farming activities.

'Yes…' Billy said as a bait for more information.

'What do you grow?'

Billy sighed and sat on his bed, forcing a squeak from it. His lips tried to form an answer but his entire voice system had frozen. He heard Sam slam the door and winced.

'Damn the police,' Billy said to himself, his beard suffering from a heavy pull.

For the first time Sam cursed Billy as he walked home: 'The fool… what a bloody selfish fool!'

At the office Billy dialled a direct line – 733004. He hadn't slept a wink last night. What game was Chinangwa playing now?

'Sosola Enterprises, good morning,' a lady's voice answered.

'Sorry, wrong number.' He hung up and dialled the number again.

'Sosola Enterprises, good morning,' the same voice on the line. Billy hesitated, a little confused. 'Can I help you?'

'What number is that?'

'What number are you dialling?' the lady asked.

'733004.'

'This is it. Who would you like to speak to?'

'Hm… well, wrong number.' Then as an afterthought, 'How long have you had this number?'

'Oh for years – a long time.'

He hung up. He dialled the next number 730544.

'Headquarters,' a voice answered at the other end, this time male. 'Can I help you?'

'Inspector Chinangwa please.'

'I am afraid he is out of the country,' the voice answered.

'But I spoke to him yesterday.'

'I said he is not in the country. Can I refer you to his assistant?'

'No, that won't be necessary.' Billy rushed to block that avenue. 'When is he coming back?'

'I don't know. Look, is this official? I could refer you to another officer if I knew your problem.'

'Personal. This is *personal*.' Billy emphasised *personal* because he suspected there was not a grain of truth in what he had just been told. He put the receiver down quietly. So Chinangwa had dumped his direct line!

He walked out to Sam's office and found him on the phone. He remained standing as a hint of the urgency of his mission. Sam was quick to pick up the hint and excused himself, promising to call later.

'These people who came last night,' Billy started. 'Are they from here?'

'No, from the south,' Sam said. 'Their accent. They can't

be from the centre.' You see if you have lived in Lilongwe as long as Sam, you can pick any Chichewa accent that was from down south or up north.

'The bastards,' Billy had now got the full picture. 'You haven't seen them here before?'

'No. I know most of the locals here. That's certainly a Blantyre team.'

Sam was dying to tell this man off for having acted so stupidly. But he dared not test his friend's temper now.

'This had to happen, Billy.' That's all Sam could afford under the circumstances.

Billy was silent.

'You know you were playing with fire. But then you wouldn't have listened if I had said anything.'

'You mean you knew all this time?'

Sam nodded.

Billy started for the door.

'Is there anything I can do?' Sam asked.

'I don't want you mixed up in this, Sam,' Billy said. 'Already they must be suspecting you. And you have been a good friend to me.' Sam was moved to tears. He was not used to seeing Billy in a defeated position, whatever his weaknesses. Billy had always been as good as a brother to him.

'Get a lawyer, Billy.'

'The trouble is I don't know who's or what's coming. I don't know who is after me. They are operating in the dark. And they are controlling the game, and all.'

At a time like this, Billy could still afford to be philosophical, much to Sam's amazement. On such occasions Sam simply adored, perhaps revered, him. What wasted and stifled talent, he would lament.

Chapter Three

After the evening meal, during which his father had been chatty about the nobility of the medical profession without really knowing what he was talking about, they sat facing each other across the coffee table.

'You must have heard things,' Baba started, followed by a cough and a slight shifting in his chair.

Khumbo also fidgeted in his chair and clasped his hands as if to announce that he, too, was ready for a serious talk.

'I will talk about your mother alone because she herself planted evil in this house.'

'But Baba…!'

'Now, my son,' he cut his son short, pointing a finger at him. 'You will not interrupt me.' He paused as if to let the message sink in. 'You will not interrupt me if you want to hear the story from me.' There followed silence.

'You will not interrupt me.'

Khumbo waited in mute amazement, shocked to discover the old short-tempered father springing back into the present. The command, the finger, the quivering lips, were all a part of his past, a part of a childhood he would be glad to leave behind permanently.

'I don't know why she did it. But for nine months I worked hard for a child we were going to have. For nine months we prepared like we had four times before, counting days, weeks and months. In hospital I stood in the waiting room sharing her anxiety. And when the baby came... do you know what it was?'

Khumbo shook his head, now realising that there must have been something tragically wrong, judging by his father's agony. The pain was as real now as the anger was bitter before.

'It was white...' he moaned, reliving the horror of the discovery on the day the news was broken to him. 'Not even an albino. Just white.'

'Oh, Christ!' Khumbo uttered blasphemously, something he regretted as soon as Baba winced. Baba did not rebuke him though.

'She sent the nurse to tell me the baby was white.' Baba was not a man to give in to tears. So he just gazed blankly at the paraffin lamp.

'She has never stepped into this house again since that day.' Baba continued. 'Thank God I wasn't allowed to touch that white child. I don't know what I would have been telling you now.'

'Where is she now?' Khumbo ventured, the tremor in his voice taking him by surprise. His ten fingers were locked and they cracked in protest against the stifling evening revelations.

Baba shook his head and continued staring at the lamp. The reflection of the little flame was very clear on Baba's eyeballs. This was the night of the lamp. Electricity had failed the small town.

'What about Paweme and Ellen?' Khumbo asked, once again attempting to reach for a thread that would connect him to some family without necessarily being part of the tragedy.

'I don't know. They gave her custody of the children.'

'But you were not in the wrong!' suggested Khumbo ineffectively.

'I refused to appear in court,' Baba went on, a very fatigued man, suddenly the facial protrusions and grey hair made sense, finding their place in the dark story.

'Your uncles made a mountain of their matrilineal case, my alleged brutality, and accused me of obscenities I cannot repeat to you. I will never look back.'

Khumbo stood up to peep through the curtain partitions into the darkness outside, thereby releasing his interlocking fingers. When he turned round, he eyed his father affectionately, admiring him for his strength, for surviving a storm that would have sunk many, himself included.

There was no sound for the following three or four minutes. Baba continued gazing at the lamp, while Khumbo continued to stare at the darkness outside as if too embarrassed by the revelations of the night to face reflections of the flame in Baba's eyes.

'Where is the headmaster's house?' Khumbo asked after a long time.

'You won't find him.'

'No, he said he would be home,' answered Khumbo.

'You have already met him?' Then after a pause, 'I guess you must be drinking too. Those who meet your brother can't believe he was brought up by me. You can hate me for saying it over and over. But you can't achieve anything in this world if you are undisciplined.'

Khumbo stood up again and disappeared into his bedroom where he changed into jeans and a casual shirt. His father remained in his chair as if there was no movement in the house. When he walked back into the sitting-room, he paused in the doorway as he studied the lonely figure of his father. It was as if a king had lost his throne to a disrespectful, power-hungry queen.

'I am sorry, son. I still don't keep beer in the house.' Baba said without looking up or turning. Khumbo proceeded to the door. 'I never will. Old-fashioned, that's what they all say.'

'Baba, where is the headmaster's house?' Khumbo asked again, hating himself for it, but having no alternative.

'It's still the house near the school,' Baba said, his voice betraying exhaustion.

Of course, thought Khumbo, annoyed with himself. 'Go to sleep, Baba,' he said as he opened the door. 'I will be a while. There are a few things I want to discuss with Mr Kalawe.'

He closed the door and walked into the darkness, thankful that he had been to the school earlier.

Pempho was home and already in bed.

Khumbo was yet to get used to retiring to bed early. In a community free of TV influence, people tended to retire early. Alternatively, and more frequently, the men spent their evenings in clubs and bars, leaving their women to be entertained by the only national medium, the radio. Slowly, Khumbo had observed, affluent families were becoming proud owners of videos and that constituted the only 'TV' in Malawi. Consequently, tape lending had become a booming business and, as usual, the Indians were already ahead in this enterprise.

It took a loud knock on the door before Pempho could respond and start dressing.

'Who is it?' he shouted from inside.

'Me, Khumbo.'

'Oh!' He then quickly unlocked and opened the door.

'Come in. I am sorry, I didn't expect you tonight.'

'Thanks. I had to change plans, seeing that I didn't have much else to do. I hope you don't mind.'

'Don't let that worry you,' Khumbo received a pat on the shoulder to assure him that he hadn't done anything wrong in coming. 'Let me get my shoes and then we'll sort ourselves out.'

Pempho disappeared into the bedroom, where there

were a few exchanges in low tones. Then a woman emerged who knelt before Khumbo, extending her hand.

'That's my wife, Irene,' Pempho shouted from the bedroom, and then he followed into the room carrying a pair of black shoes. 'Now, my wife, this is the much-talked-about Dr Khumbo Dala. Take all your ailments to him and your cure is guaranteed.'

'He was my classmate here, something like fifteen years ago,' Pempho continued as the two shook hands,

'It's a long time,' agreed Khumbo as his forehead furrowed instantly on recollecting how badly Pempho had reacted to this comment on time.

'Irene was a baby then,' Pempho said and she giggled at the remark without any protest. To Khumbo's relief, Pempho didn't take much notice of his comment about time.

'She used to come from Mtengo village escorted by a bully of a brother.'

'He wasn't a bully,' she protested finally, laughing as she rose from her knees and sat on a chair at the table facing the wall so that their visitor was not directly opposite her. Women just didn't look men in the eye.

'He was,' insisted Pempho, and then turning to Khumbo, 'you remember Zuze?'

'Yes,' Khumbo answered and smothered a roaring laugh. 'Zuze Khama!'

'Tell her, Khumbo,' Pempho said, his huge body heaving with laughter. 'She doesn't believe me. Tell her.'

'No, that's all forgotten now,' Khumbo couldn't contain his laughter any more. And then he started coughing.

'She ought to know.' And so Pempho continued adding fuel to the leaping flames of merriment. 'Khumbo was the youngest in the class, but I must hasten to add the naughtiest. So on this day under discussion, the D.C.'s son was feeling particularly naughty. So he stood up and started: "There will be a football match at break time – town versus village. All villagers form a team and we town boys will form a team." Zuze jumped to grab him by the neck and was only stopped by the other equally big boys. Khumbo ran home for his ball at break and the game was under way in no time at all. By the time the bell went the town boys were two-nil up. You should have seen the chase. The big villagers chasing the rude tiny town boys… And guess who Zuze went after?' The laughter was at its loudest.

'It took two big boys to pull Zuze away from little Khumbo, but not before he had drawn blood from the poor boy.' He paused.

'Khumbo, finish the story.'

'No, you are already through,' Khumbo replied.

'Tell her what happened to her brother.'

'Leave my brother alone,' Irene protested amidst laughter. 'He must be choking wherever he is.' These silly boys, she thought teasingly. 'You shouldn't mention a person at night. It brings them bad luck, often tripping as they walked or choking as they ate.'

'He will choke all right,' Pempho's enjoyment of the

story was total. 'He will choke now that his victim is back. A full medical doctor.'

'Okay,' Irene yielded. 'What happened to him?'

'Wasn't he expelled?' Khumbo asked in a genuine effort to remember, amazed by how much of the incident had actually faded from memory.

'Now you are with us,' agreed Pempho.

'Anyway,' started Irene as if to close the chapter. 'He still went on to become an engineer.'

'Engineer?' Khumbo exclaimed.

'Oh, yah! Khumbo,' Pempho confirmed. 'He is now with the Electricity Supply Commission as an electrical engineer.'

'I can't believe it,' said Khumbo.

'You better,' Irene answered proudly, stealing a victorious look at Khumbo.

'I am the only one who didn't make it.' It was Pempho's turn to hold the prickly end of the stick. 'Everywhere I go, this one is now a doctor, a lecturer, an engineer, or a manager or... or a minister. Yes, of course you know who. I don't have to mention names. And look at me: "Headmaster!"'

'Oh, *aPhiri*,' pleaded Irene, calling Pempho by his clan name as a way of appeasing the offended ego. 'Don't start again. We can't all have the same things. I am merely a primary school teacher.'

'Of course you are. And where does that place me?' Pempho asked, somewhat irritated by the comparison.

'Among women, eh? First among women, that's what I am.'

'I am sorry, doctor,' Irene said. 'But we tend to get into these silly arguments so often now. I just can't cope. I will retire to bed.'

'And good riddance too,' concluded Pempho. Turning to Khumbo, he said, 'Let's go.'

'Where?' Khumbo asked, amazed.

'For a drink.'

'No. I just came for a chat,' Khumbo said, hoping that Pempho's wounds could be balmed without necessarily going out. 'Can't we leave that for tomorrow?'

'My friend,' Pempho was already opening the door. 'There is no entertainment I can offer you here. I can't even play you music. You want to listen to "Radio Quiz"? Come, we will have a chat as we go. At the pub we will have more time.'

'What the heck!' Khumbo said with resignation and stood up to join Pempho outside. Pempho locked the door.

'You are not locking her in?' asked Khumbo.

'I have to,' Pempho replied. 'She prefers that to waking up and opening the door at 3 a.m.'

Khumbo followed his friend in silence. After a while he asked: 'You know about my mother, don't you?' Khumbo was in a hurry to get as much information as he could before getting to the bar.

'Yes,' Pempho replied. 'I am sorry about that. Everybody knows about it.'

'Where is she?'

Pempho went quiet for a minute, taking care not to pierce wounds already there.

'In Salima,' Pempho said eventually. 'Ask for Gona Pano Motel. It's very popular there.'

Khumbo wanted to ask more questions, but preferred not to since his friend seemed unwilling to engage in a detailed discussion. They went on in silence until they were greeted by the blaring ill-mixed sounds from the *gumbagumba*.

It took Khumbo and Pempho a whole hour before they could warm to the festive mood in the bar. There was hardly enough room on the dance floor as the DJ spinned one rumba number after another. Interestingly, for Khumbo at least, the local artists too had swung from the predominantly *simanjemanje* beat of the early seventies to the 'now' rumba sound. In the bustle, jostling and chit-chat that accompanied the music, it was not easy to tell which rumba sound was local, and which imported. It was only when the vocals were listened to with a keen ear that the distinction could be made.

Pempho was easily a local celebrity, judging by the number of invitations to the floor – to which he gave a polite but firm 'no'. Sometimes a gesture was all he needed and the girl would go smarting away. Sometimes he had to explain.

'I am not in a dancing mood,' he would say.

'What's wrong today?' the girl would ask, almost certain that this was the usual tough-guy attitude and he was bound to come out of it. It was amazing how the night and pub atmosphere so readily transformed the day-time docile and humble female into an aggressive equal of the male.

'Today I have an important visitor,' he would answer. 'This is Dr Khumbo Dala.' She would then pop her eyes out of their drunken sockets and fix a look at Khumbo.

'So, you see,' Pempho would now deal the final blow. 'He is not for cheap stuff like you.'

That would send her away muttering obscenities which would luckily drown in the buzz of the dancing floor.

'You don't have to be so nasty,' Khumbo corrected him at one time.

'You try to be gentle and see where you end up,' he challenged Khumbo. 'By the way, Khumbo, you didn't tell me what you think about my teacher, Grace Ndele?'

'Oh, so her name is Grace?' Khumbo asked naughtily.

'What do you think of her?' persisted Pempho.

'I will answer that question if you promise to go and get her to dance with me.'

Pempho considered the proposal.

'No, best not to bring her here,' Pempho advised.

'Why not?' asked Khumbo. 'You are not scared of her, big Pempho?'

'She won't come here. We have all tried. She won't.'

Then as an afterthought, 'Why not buy the beer and take it to her place?'

'Why not?'

Before long they had half a dozen bottles of beer tucked under their armpits as they walked back to the school where most of the teachers' houses were.

'So what do you think of her?' Pempho continued his enquiry.

'Cut it out, will you?' Khumbo said, laughing.

'Well, well, well,' Pempho concluded. 'Watch this page is what the newspaper man said.'

'Tell me about mother,' Khumbo returned to the more substantial topic of the night.

'I can't tell you much,' Pempho replied rather evasively. 'I was here less than a year when it all happened. Why not ask the old man?'

'I can't stand it, hearing him talk about it.'

'Well, she has done well for herself.'

'How? By getting a divorce?'

'No, not that.'

'I wish somebody could tell me something about my mother.' Khumbo burst out. 'Even my brother won't tell me anything. What if I walk into mother's house and there is a man... I mean has she remarried?'

'It's none of my business, Khumbo,' Pempho said, rather disconcerted by it all. 'These things happen in life. I grew up without a father. It's up to you if you wish to take sides. I just don't know what to say. Look...'

'Let's leave it at that. I thought you…'

'You thought I would go around gathering stories about your parents? Khumbo, I wish you could understand…'

They stopped outside one of the houses in a straight line separated from the school by the football ground. There was no light in any of them.

Pempho knocked several times before he could get any response.

'Who is it?' she called from the bedroom.

'The headmaster,' Pempho replied.

There was a long silence and a lamp was lit before she came round to unlock the door. She opened just enough to show her face while lifting the lamp above her head to have a clear view of the visitor.

'Can I help you?' she enquired somewhat bashfully.

'The doctor and I thought you could keep us company as we…' Pempho lifted the bottles to finish his sentence.

'But sir,' she lisped her protest, 'you know I don't drink.'

'You won't drink.' Then noticing his mistake, 'Oh, no!' Khumbo lifted his arms to look at the bottles as if to say how unfortunate. He lowered his arms as soon as he realised that no excuse would make him any cleverer.

'Tell you what I'll do,' Pempho suggested. 'I'll run back. What will you drink?'

'Coke,' replied Miss Ndele.

Before Khumbo and Miss Ndele grasped the significance of his suggestion, Pempho had already disappeared, leaving three bottles on the doorstep.

'In that case you can come in,' volunteered Miss Ndele.

'I can wait here if that's more convenient,' Khumbo said, finding the whole episode a bit disconcerting. Now he wasn't certain whether it was genuine forgetfulness on the part of Pempho.

'Oh, do come in before the neighbours start talking,' she said as she opened the door wide and retreated inside. The neighbours! That was some story. By that she meant the womenfolk. Would they leave a single girl alone in this little town? No, she must be greedy if she can't get married. No, it's her education. No, you are wrong: she has so many boyfriends, she doesn't know who to choose. And so on…

Khumbo entered and placed his three bottles down before returning to the door for Pempho's. Miss Ndele had already disappeared into the bedroom. When she came out she was carrying a bottle opener. She opened one bottle and offered it to Khumbo.

'Here you are, doctor,' she said, offering the opener.

'Call me Khumbo if you don't mind,' Khumbo found this a very convenient starting point.

'What happens when Mrs Dala hears me calling you by your first name?' She wouldn't let important questions wait.

'Which Mrs Dala?' he asked, very flabbergasted.

'You don't expect me to believe that at your age you don't have anybody feeling jealous for you,' she continued, to provoke some committed statement. Khumbo's face was immediately invaded by furrows.

'Oh, you mean…' Khumbo couldn't finish.

'You don't expect me to be scared of your mother?'

Khumbo laughed loudly, enjoying her sense of humour. Even this reference to his mother did not bother him.

'No, there is no Mrs Dala to be afraid of,' he assured her. 'Now you can call me Khumbo.'

'Okay,' she said smiling. 'I believe you.'

'Can I call you Grace?' he begged.

'How do you know my name?' she quizzed lightheartedly.

'I have done my research,' he said. 'Go on, prove me wrong.'

'Call me Grace, if that makes you feel better.'

'It won't make me feel any better if you don't join me in my drink.'

'Well, I don't drink beer.'

'I am not the headmaster, you know,' Khumbo was feeling more and more relaxed. Her smile was totally disarming, and her lips melodious. 'I won't report you either.'

'He won't come back, you can be sure of that,' Grace said with the confidence of a woman who knew her men.

'How do you know that?' he asked.

'This is not the first time he has done this to me,' she replied. 'That's the price you pay for being single in a small town like this. Everyone is making passes at you.'

Khumbo was quiet for some time, trying to get the significance of this statement.

'Don't get me wrong, doctor… Khumbo,' she went on after noticing Khumbo's sudden reticence. 'With you it's different. What I don't understand is why you wouldn't wait till tomorrow. Look, I can't even offer you a meal.'

'Well, I had to find something to do, and then Pempho suggested having a drink and I suggested your company, and so on. Before we knew it we were here.' Khumbo hoped this explained his unpredictability.

'Wait a minute,' Grace said. 'Who suggested me?'

'I did, why?'

'It can't be,' said Grace incredulously.

'It's true,' Khumbo said, yielding. 'Why, you don't expect me to want to see you?'

'No, it's not that,' she said. 'The visitors I have had from Pempho have always come at Pempho's instigation.' She then hesitated before proceeding. 'It's as if he wants to see my breaking point.'

'Well, this one came of his own accord. His invitation is for tomorrow, remember?' Khumbo reminded her.

'Tomorrow?' she feigned surprise.

'Don't tell me you have forgotten already,' Khumbo wondered.

'I don't take him seriously, you know,' she said tantalisingly.

'Will you take me seriously, then?'

'Depends on what you ask of me,' she said.

'Have a little drink with me,' he suggested again. 'Let me open a bottle for you.'

'No, I don't drink. But, then, that doesn't mean I haven't taken your offer seriously,' she explained.

'If I suggested another meeting tomorrow, would you take me seriously?'

'Yes,' she answered.

'Where?'

'Same place. I don't go out with strangers.' She volunteered the last piece of information.

'Why? Afraid of them?'

'It's the gossip in town,' she explained. 'They see you with a stranger and conclusions are drawn and broadcast.'

'I thought it was just another jealous guy you were afraid of,' he suggested.

'That too is a factor to reckon with,' she said, laughing.

'Who is he?' He pressed on.

'Let me worry about him,' she said firmly.

Silence followed except for Khumbo's noisy gulps of beer.

'Can I make a suggestion?' she asked.

'Feel free.'

'Would you consider me rude if I asked you to come back tomorrow?' she asked fearfully.

'Of course not,' he protested.

'You see, I feel silly entertaining you without offering you anything,' she apologised.

'You needn't bother,' he tried to quell her fears. 'But. I appreciate your position.'

She was expressing every woman's worry. Beauty aside, a woman's potential as a wife was judged by her ability to cook and entertain. The day she entertained her suitor and his representatives is the day she got endorsed as acceptable. Sometimes the judgement would be received through hints, sometimes directly. From then on word would spread that the daughter of so and so may be beautiful, but she will starve your son and his relations.

'Why don't you have supper here tomorrow?' she offered.

'Since you say you won't take Pempho's invitation seriously, I can only say I'll be delighted.'

'Thank you very much,' she sighed with relief. 'That really makes me feel better.'

He rose to go and realised that he had four bottles still unopened.

'Can I leave them here?' he asked, and then corrected himself immediately. 'I'm sorry, you have no fridge. I'll take them with me.' He felt awkward for making this remark.

'No, I can keep them here and exchange them for cold ones at the bottlestore tomorrow,' she said. She knew a shopkeeper who was kind enough to let her use his refrigerator as and when she needed one.

'Can you?' he asked, relieved. 'I don't want to be a burden.'

'Not at all. That is, if you won't need them tonight.'

'I won't,' he said. 'I swear,' he added to answer her naughty smile.

'Then I'll keep them. How many do you drink in one night?' she went on to ask.

'Those are enough for one night,' he said.
'Good. That means I don't have to buy beer.'
They laughed.
'Good night, then,' he said as he opened the door.
'Good night.'

As Khumbo turned in his old bed, he found his sleep disturbed by its squeak. He made efforts to quieten it by lying on his stomach, and that's when he felt the urgency to go to the toilet – it just couldn't be postponed. He cursed silently and jumped out of the blankets, put on his robe, and went out.

'Mwadzuka bwanji, bwana?' Kachala greeted him, enquiring about his health.

'Ndadzuka bwino kaya inu?' Khumbo returned the greeting, enquiring after Kachala's health, and disappeared into the toilet before the conversation got out of hand.

When he came out, a much happier man, he walked to the kitchen door, where he learnt that Baba had already left for the office. He looked at his watch: 9.30. He hadn't heard a sound. He chose to blame the heat rather than the beer. He was sure he could take more than he took last night and still be his bouncing self.

'Breakfast, *bwana*?' Kachala enquired.
'Do you have coffee?' asked Khumbo.
'No. Your father drinks tea only,' Kachala explained.

'Come and get some money and buy me coffee and a packet of razor blades.'

Khumbo went back into the house and slipped into his blankets. He had just dozed off when he was awakened by a loud knock. He waited some minutes hoping Kachala was already back from the grocery so that he would answer the knock. But as there was no sound other than the rapping on the door, he dragged himself out and walked dazedly through the sitting-room to open the door. It was Pempho.

'You have forty-five minutes to make it to the assembly, big boy,' Pempho said.

'What are you talking about?'

'Our appointment with those unambitious souls so that when they see a local descend on them from a London-based Boeing 747 they might have another crack at those sums, etc.'

'Oh!' Khumbo moaned, feeling his nagging head with the palm of his right hand while ridges appeared on his forehead. 'Do come in. I haven't had breakfast.'

'No. You have your breakfast. I said forty-five minutes. I can make it an hour if you like.'

'That's better,' said Khumbo. 'Now get going and I'll see you in an hour.'

'Late night, eh?' asked Pempho naughtily before closing the door.

'It's not what you think,' Khumbo shouted after the door had banged closed. 'The bastard!' he said to himself as he rummaged through his suitcase for formal wear.

Chapter Four

The assembly turned out to be the same old multi-purpose mango tree. When assembly met the teachers sat under it whilst the pupils sat on the football pitch facing the platform. During matches pupils mixed freely with their teachers as they all sought protection from the sun or drizzle. Khumbo sat between Pempho and Grace, although he made sure that conversation between the lady and himself was reduced to the barest minimum. The scene before him could have moved anyone with memories of childhood that were connected with the school: khaki shorts and shirts for boys and green dresses with white collars for girls, bare and dusty feet. The only difference was the replacement of 'English khaki', originally imported from Manchester, with locally manufactured material.

The headmaster stood up.

'Today we are privileged to have in our midst Dr Khumbo Dala who has just arrived from England. Dr Dala went to school here. In fact he was my classmate and together we sat under this mango tree in the same position as you are now. But his vision was greater than ours – certainly greater than mine!' This prompted laughter from the children and the staff as well. To Khumbo's amazement there was some whistling accompanying the laughter which went unadmonished.

'You, you can laugh,' Pempho continued. 'We did not have any ambition. Our future and ambition were all confined to this little town. And that's why I am still here. For this reason I have requested Dr Dala to speak to us about achievement, success, etc., so that you are put on the right track. What he has achieved started here, and I want him to assure you that there are doctors, engineers, and lawyers among you, if only you have ambition.'

'Dr Dala, please address your former school.'

There was a loud clap as Khumbo stood up, instantly making him gigantic among helpless children. He had chosen to wear a navy blue double-breasted jacket and a pair of grey trousers. A white shirt matched the trousers, while a blue and white dotted necktie matched the jacket. There was something wrong about him standing in front just to frustrate the children. He thought of the depressing world economic situation and wondered what was right about raising the hopes of these innocents.

'When I was your age,' Khumbo started. 'I did not have toys. For us to play football we had to roll banana leaves into a ball. It used to hurt, but that's all we had. In schools we used sisal to weave strings and mats. We made hoes and wooden stools. But all the time we did those things half-heartedly, dreaming of the day we would all do something better. Some of us dreamt of getting away from here for ever. Well, that was a solution then. Now things have changed. There are more of us and fewer jobs in the city. Now young ones like you need to learn a skill and make more hoes and mats.

'How many of you have been to the big cities – Blantyre, and Lilongwe?' he asked. Two hands went up.

'It means most of you haven't been out of this little town. I'll tell you something about Lilongwe.

'There are many young men earning a living from craft. They paint animals, portraits, or buildings and sell them. They carve objects from wood and stone. Some mould statues. But more interestingly, some are selling children's toys: tricycles, cars, and aeroplanes.

'So you see, we can't all be doctors. As long as we prepare ourselves to lead an independent life – and we are not begging – we should be satisfied with our endeavours. Mr Kalawe here is doing what he has prepared himself to do in life. I can't teach and that's why I chose to be a doctor. So among you will be doctors, craftsmen, teachers, farmers. As long as you are satisfied with your choice, let nothing else distract you from your goal.'

He paused and searched his mind for anything to add. He then wondered whether he hadn't been speaking above their heads.

'Who has a question?' A hand went up. 'Yes?'

'You didn't tell us about England,' a boy said after standing up.

'No, I didn't,' Khumbo answered, thrown off balance.

He had deliberately left out that subject with the intention of motivating them into working hard and making realistic career choices without reference to his overseas experience.

'Do they all wear suits?' asked another.

'Is it true that they all have cars?'

Pempho jumped to his feet; 'Quiet! let's have order. John, Lucy, sit down. Where is the head prefect? Prefects take names of those who speak without authority.'

He then turned to Khumbo and said hastily: 'Listen, you fool, what they want to hear about is London, New York, and millionaires. They know enough about poverty – you don't have to preach that to them.' Then he turned to the pupils. 'What Dr Dala is telling you is true. So behave yourselves. Of course he will tell you about England. But only if you behave yourselves.'

He then returned to his seat, leaving Khumbo rooted to his spot.

'England,' Khumbo started again, hesitantly. 'England is not a big country. Mostly white. There are blacks like you who are from islands called the West Indies and some from Africa, mostly West Africa. There are also Asians from India, Pakistan, Bangladesh, and other Asian countries. There are rich and poor people. You see, being white does not always mean being rich. Some own cars, some don't. Some have suits, others don't. Some work in offices, others work as drivers or garbage collectors…'

He was interrupted by loud and noisy laughter.

'It's true. Otherwise who do you think collects garbage for them?'

'Machines!' yelled one. Pempho decided not to intervene. Khumbo too thought it was an innocent comment.

'No. The garbage trucks are driven by people. The bins are lifted and their contents emptied into the trucks by men. And this is an example of how everybody can be useful in the community. The garbage collectors, drivers, businessmen, doctors, teachers, and farmers are all important in their different ways.

'In the big city of London where I was, it is easier to travel by bus, underground train, or taxi. Since you all know about buses and taxis, let me tell you about underground trains. The train is called the tube as well. Since it is faster to travel by tube, many people leave their cars at home and use the trains to get to work, school or market.'

The silence astounded him. His was the only voice in the openness that engulfed him. Except for the birds chirping above, whose droppings could be seen on a skirt or a head or a shoulder. Also chickens from the teachers' houses could be seen wandering about freely, searching for insects. At a distance a chicken was attempting to extract itself from a determined cockerel.

'It's no longer unusual for blacks and whites to marry. In London it is common for whites and blacks to marry.'

'Is your wife a *mzungu*?' The question came back and it seemed to stir the gathering into some amused excitement.

'I am not married yet…' he started and then changed

his mind. His experience might be worth a dozen books or a thousand lectures on multi-racial Britain.

'I have a fiancée who is white. Her name is Miss Susan Kelly. She is also a doctor and we have lived together for the past four years…'

'Your wife is white then!' It was a girl this time.

He looked at her before responding. The significance of his revelation on the children and morals was overwhelming.

'You better tell them she is your wife,' he heard Pempho from behind. 'How else do you explain your living together?'

'Yes, my wife is white,' he found himself saying, as if accepting a verdict he had employed all the renowned legal practitioners to prevent.

'Can she cook *nsima*?' The girl was standing tall among her mates as she articulated in her question the worries of those who surrounded her, as well as Baba's and possibly his mother's. What is a wife if she can't cook *nsima*? How do you live with a woman if she isn't your wife?

'No, she cannot cook our *nsima*,' he said as he recomposed himself. 'But she can cook their own *nsima* and I have learnt to love it. You see, different people eat different food.'

There were no more questions. One would have thought that the confession had done the trick, that what he had been saying before had been impersonal and fictitious. The advent of tangible events surrounding people they knew seemed to have brought down to earth the experience that had hitherto hinged on fantasy and heaven. Dr Dala plus Miss Susan Kelly plus *nsima* suddenly made the stories real and within human grasp. Some of them saw themselves on a jumbo jet crossing the large seas to live with and among strangers: whites, blacks, or Asians.

Then he felt a hand on his shoulder.

'Well done,' Pempho said with a big smile spreading across his face.

'Thank you,' Khumbo replied. 'Can I sit down now?'

'Not yet,' Pempho replied as he went on to address the assembly.

'I think we will now ask Dr Dala to sit down. But before he does so, I would like to thank him on everybody's behalf for sparing his precious time to come and talk to us. I am sure you agree with me that through him we have come closer to England. To express our gratitude, I will ask you to stand and give him a big hand.'

They gave him a deafening hand, which did not include whistling. He bowed and sat down. The staff joined him in sitting down while the children were dismissed for the rest of the morning.

Khumbo hadn't noticed Grace's absence until he saw her coming back followed by a boy carrying a crate of soft drinks.

'I am sorry, we don't allow beer on the school premises,' Pempho explained as the crate was placed down.

'What will you have?' Grace asked Khumbo.

'Fanta, please,' he said, followed by 'Thank you' as soon as he had received his drink.

Afterwards, Grace came back to stand where Khumbo was standing, talking to Irene. Irene excused herself.

'You don't have any more secrets now, do you?' Grace asked.

'Meaning?' Khumbo asked, somewhat perplexed.

'Well, it appears there is somebody guarding the doctor jealously after all,' she pursued her point teasingly.

'No comment,' said Khumbo, sipping his Fanta.

'Well, what have you got to say for yourself?' she quizzed persistently.

'Do you want a story?' Khumbo asked, irritated. He walked away towards Pempho.

'See you this evening,' she said, following him.

'I will think about it,' he said, and then turned. 'Now can you leave me alone?'

'Not until you have thought about it and given me your decision,' she said rather aggressively.

'You aren't worth even a second look,' he said, now turning to head for home, really angry with himself and everybody.

Grace walked back towards the rest and met Pempho where they could not be heard.

'What's wrong with him now?' he asked her.

'You go and ask him,' she retorted. 'And don't you dare bring that arrogant he-goat to my house again.'

'Wait a minute…' he made an attempt to calm her.

'There is no point creating a scene here,' she reasoned with him in spite of her fury. 'There is your wife, the school children and your staff. I don't think he is worth all that fuss. Do you?'

With that she walked away in the direction of her house. Pempho issued the last orders to his staff and excused himself in order to catch up with Dr Dala and see him home. When he caught up with him, he didn't know how to start a conversation.

'Shall I walk you home?' he asked Khumbo.

'It's not necessary,' Khumbo answered, and then changed to a more conciliatory course. 'But you are quite welcome if you have nothing better to do.'

'Oh, that's better.' Pempho was pleased with the results of his diplomacy. 'Are you coming tonight?' Khumbo did not reply; he just walked on.

'By the way,' Pempho tried again. 'What did you say to Grace?'

'What about?' Khumbo snapped back.

'I don't know. She just sounded upset. I met her soon after she had spoken to you,' Pempho suggested.

'Why can't you mind your own business? Does she have to know how many women I've had in my life just because I visited her last night?' Pointing a trembling finger at Pempho, he said: 'And next time don't trick me into those situations!'

'Wait a minute,' Pempho interrupted. 'It was your idea in the first place. All I wanted last night was a drink.'

'Then why did you have to lie about going back for drinks?'

'You didn't expect me to preside over your tête-à-tête?' asked Pempho seriously. 'Listen, if things haven't worked out between you two, just too bad, but don't push the blame on to me.'

'Then don't ask me questions about it,' Khumbo warned.

'Fine,' Pempho agreed. 'Excuse me, I have to go.'

Pempho returned to his office after seeing Khumbo home. Khumbo entered his room and threw himself on the bed. Several minutes later he returned to the sitting-room and sat down to read an old *Newsweek* magazine his father had kept. There was a knock. When he opened the door, he found himself staring into Grace's eyes.

'I've come to apologise,' she said. Still Khumbo just stared at her.

'I had no right to probe,' she continued. 'I am so sorry.' She turned to go and stopped just before going down the steps.

'Please do come to dinner this evening?'

'What do you hope to achieve?' He spoke at last.

'I've spent the whole night imagining what having dinner with you would be like. You see, in this place it's not easy to find exciting company. Don't spoil it for me, please.'

'I've already packed my suitcase,' he said.

'Going already?' she asked, disappointed. 'Is that how bad you feel about us?'

'Going to see my mother,' he said.

'Can't she wait until tomorrow?' she pleaded. 'Does she know you are coming today?'

'No.'

'Then do stay the night. After that you can go.'

He looked past her at the houses in the distance and, farther than that, at the big volume of water in the lake, all this while aware of her unflinching gaze. Then she turned and disappeared round the house.

'Kachala!' he called after several minutes of indecision.

'*Bwana!*' Kachala answered and ran into the house.

'Has Miss Ndele gone far?' asked Khumbo.

'I can find her, *bwana*,' Kachala promised.

'Call her for me, will you?' He didn't need to say any more, for Kachala had already disappeared. Shortly she knocked again.

'Come in,' he shouted.

The door squeaked open and she entered timidly, like an offending dog whose tail has already been tucked between the legs as an admission of his guilt.

'Have a seat,' he said, pointing to a chair next to his.

'Thank you,' she muttered inaudibly.

'I am sorry,' he started, his hands gesturing aimlessly until they hung limply about him.

'It's understandable,' she said. 'I provoked you.'

'I don't want to discuss it here. My father will be here shortly. How about going for a drive this afternoon?' he enquired. This time it was his turn to tuck his tail between his legs for fear of rejection which might shatter his male ego. In that flash of a second his fingers locked, the knuckles cracked, and the furrows dug deeper and deeper into his forehead.

'Where?' she enquired in a non-committal tone.

'Nowhere. Just around,' he explained, although deep down he nursed a secret desire to end up inside the waters of the deep, blue lake in the distance.

'Well, since I don't have to cook any more I don't see why not,' she said naughtily.

'What do you mean you don't have to cook? You mean we'll come back to uncooked chicken?'

By this time she knew where she stood. She rose to go, thinking to herself, 'Why do you men have to be so proud all the time?'

'What time?' she asked walking to the door.

'What time do you finish in the afternoon?'

'Three-thirty,' she answered.

'Three-thirty, then,' he concluded.

'I'll meet you here,' she said with an air of finality.

Khumbo knocked on Pempho's door and entered as soon as he received an answer from inside.

'I need some boys to help me push the car,' Khumbo said desperately. 'It won't start.'

'Let me see if there is anybody around,' Pempho said, rising from his chair. 'Why didn't you come earlier?'

'I didn't know it wouldn't start.'

'Well, there may still be some pupils on punishment,' Pempho said as he went out, followed by a very frustrated Khumbo. Four boys were cutting grass.

'Okay, boys,' the headmaster commanded. 'Go with Dr Dala. He has some work for you. When you finish you can go.'

'Thank you, sir,' they said in a chorus.

It took the boys fifteen minutes to get the car rolling enough to start, by which time Grace had bitten her nails clean. She had heard so much about Baba's temper and strictness. So, when the engine finally revved, she didn't wait for an invitation to get into the car.

'Whew!' exclaimed Khumbo, 'What a bad start.'

She didn't say anything, but just looked ahead while recovering her breath. For the first time today he took in the details. All she needed was the restoration of confidence in herself, as she already knew how to capture a man's attention. She always spoke with a smile and what normally appeared as large lips would thin into total withdrawal when she laughed. Khumbo really liked what he saw sitting next to him.

'Where are we going?'

'Anywhere,' she said.

'Listen,' he cautioned, returning the smile. 'I don't know which areas are worth visiting any more. So if you don't make up your mind, we'll end up going round the little town.'

'Have you been to the factory?' she asked.

'Which factory?'

'The sugar factory,' she said.

'No, shall we try that?'

'It's worth visiting if you haven't been there before,' she advised.

'I wasn't here when it was built,' he said. 'I left when there was talk of its possibility, that's all.'

'In that case we are heading the wrong way.' He tried a U-turn and failed. It took a second attempt to complete the turn. The motorway took them through forests and bush, heading for Dwangwa. Once in a while a rabbit or squirrel would scurry across the road. The rabbit reminded him of Uncle Jumbe's hunting escapades. Often he would bring smoked meat to town to sell at the market. What he brought home almost invariably ended up stewed in groundnut gravy, a favourite dish Khumbo always associated with Uncle Jumbe. When he came from the market in the evening, he would narrate stories of how he would use his hunting dog Nyamazako to lead him to the game and how he would decide when to use a spear, a club, or Nyamazako. For example, rabbits were best captured by Nyamazako. Otherwise any attempt to use a spear or club proved foolhardy and, at times, led to loss of the dispatched weapon.

'Have you forgiven the male chauvinist?' he asked his somewhat reticent companion.

'I don't have to forgive. I've forgotten all about it.' She

continued after getting no encouragement from Khumbo, 'After all I am used to it.'

'Oh, you are?'

'My fiancé is no exception,' she revealed with a nod. 'If he were we would be married by now,' she went on. 'Imagine the selfishness of it all. He can't even make up his mind to get me out of this bush. There is no way I will find a chance to be transferred to the city until I am married.'

'I think I understand,' Khumbo remarked at last.

'At first, we were waiting for him to complete his overseas training,' she resumed her life story. 'Then he had to settle down. Now it is raising money for the big day. Deep down I am convinced it won't work.'

'Give him a chance.' Khumbo was trying to sound helpful. 'He may not be that deceptive. You know how we Malawians love big weddings: six bridesmaids, four flower girls, an equal number of bestmen. And as if paying for their dress is not enough, he has to book the best hotel in town for a reception to accommodate the whole town. I don't blame him.'

'Well, some girl there in Blantyre is bound to get pregnant!' she blurted.

'Oh, so that's the fear,' he said, rather undecided whether to sympathise or laugh about it.

'And then it'll be a choice between me and his bastard,' she concluded.

'Really?' he asked, not really expecting an answer.

Silence ensued for a while.

'I am sorry,' he said. 'I didn't expect you to have such a sombre story. You sure know how to hide your feelings.'

'In Nkhotakota, people can create stories,' she said to answer his concern. 'I cannot even confide my disappointments in anybody.'

'Why are you telling me all this, then?'

'You are an outsider,' she said calmly. 'You are bound to go away – back to the city – and forget about this silly bush girl wasting away under a mango tree.' She paused.

'But there is a better reason,' she continued. 'I haven't had a chance to say this to anybody for a long time. And somehow it didn't matter if you went ahead to discuss me with your friend Pempho. It just doesn't seem to matter.'

They had been on the motorway for something like thirty minutes when Khumbo noticed an expanse of green running parallel to Lake Malawi, and therefore parallel to the motorway. In fact it was his memory that drew the limits of the green plantation. From the road, the sugarcane stood taller and larger than any he had known before. But as the stalks disappeared into the thickness of the green plantation it no longer caused the sensation it had when he was a boy. Lost in the green thickness the sugarcane did not have the suppleness that had once made it attractive.

'I wonder if they are as sweet as our local ones,' he took the chance to change the subject.

'Those who have tasted it find it salty,' she advised. 'But then you have no way of finding out.'

'Why not?' he asked, perplexed.

'You can actually be arrested,' she said.

'For what?'

'Eating the sugarcane.'

'Impossible!' he said in disbelief.

'Try them. There is a ruling against being found eating sugarcane. And it doesn't matter where you get it from.'

'Reason?' he asked.

'There is no way the company authorities can tell which is from the plantation and which from private gardens.'

'You mean people have stopped eating their own sugarcane?'

'Exactly,' she said, unperturbed.

Khumbo stopped the car. He looked at the plantation and shook his head. He looked at Grace and puzzled over her placid acceptance of the situation.

'Grace,' he said.

'Yes, Khumbo,' she answered with unnerving calmness in her voice.

'I will walk there and pull down one cane and I will eat it here and now.'

'And what do you hope to achieve?' she asked with the same calmness.

Instead of answering her, he walked the twenty yards or so separating the road and plantation, gave the stalk a good look and started stripping one of its leaves until it stood naked, vulnerable, and virgin. He took hold of it at the top and forced it down with one jerk. It snapped at the bottom and he pulled it off its roots. He leaned it against the ground and broke it into four equal pieces and started peeling one piece with his teeth as he walked back to the car.

He leaned against the car as he chewed and sucked before spitting out the chaff.

'It is actually salty,' he pronounced his judgement. 'But I don't mind that so long as I have had Dwangwa sugarcane.'

'I think it's too early for celebration,' she cautioned, seeing a man in uniform approaching.

'*Bwana*,' there was a call from behind.

He was carrying a club in one hand and the leaves Khumbo had peeled off the cane in the other. 'Please take the leaves away with you.'

'And why would I want to do that?' he asked aggressively.

'If you leave them there, *bwana*, I will lose my job when they discover that a sugarcane has been stolen.'

Khumbo looked at him with eyes that nearly moistened.

Without a nod he reached out for the leaves and threw them into the boot.

'I am sorry, *bwana*,' he pleaded with Khumbo. 'But I don't want to make trouble for you. And I don't want to lose my job.'

Khumbo dipped into his pocket and produced a one Kwacha note which he handed to the guard.

'Thank you, *bwana*,' the guard said. 'But I am only doing my job. If this was my garden you could have eaten as much as you wanted. You could even have taken some home!' He folded the money and put it in his pocket.

Khumbo got into the car, opened his mouth with the intention of warning him not to be too kind to too many culprits if he wanted to keep his job, and then let his mouth close on second thoughts. He reversed the car and then swung it facing where they had just come from.

'But we haven't been to the factory,' Grace said.

'I've seen enough of the factory as it is.'

They drove in silence, lost in their different thoughts. Khumbo had trained himself to speak as little as possible when angry, because every time he opened his mouth in anger he ended up with more trouble than he could contain. So where there was a choice between verbal and physical confrontation, he had, as a boy, preferred the latter. Grace was not prepared for another confrontation with him. So she just watched him as he changed gears up and down the meandering road. It was only when the steam started seeping through the bonnet that she screamed.

'Fire!'

Khumbo swore and cursed under his breath as he applied the brakes, immediately realising his mistake. Having not checked the water level in the radiator, the last thing the old car needed was the kind of rough handling it had just had. He got out and opened the bonnet, leaving it open and letting the radiator cool down on its own rather than opening it. He had heard enough stories about careless drivers burning their faces from boiling squirts from overheating radiators. Grace had already run a hundred yards or so down the road, remembering the many cars she had seen in films catching fire from less serious faults. Slowly she walked back to the car.

When she arrived back on the scene, Khumbo found himself holding her hand and pulling her to him. What amazed them both was how they seemed to find refuge in each other so willingly.

'It's only a radiator,' he said soothingly, pressing her bosom against his. 'It will take an hour before it cools down.'

He held her body close to his. When he looked into her eyes, he was alarmed by the fear he saw in them, so that when their lips met he kissed her with the greatest gentleness.

He walked with her to the car and opened the rear door. When they sat down, they embraced and kissed, wildly opening to each other's hearts in a manner they had never done before. It was only after the fire had burnt itself out that they discovered the darkness which enveloped them. To their amazement, no car, no bicycle, or pedestrian had gone past to interrupt the extinguishing of fire in the two desperate bodies whose flames had leapt above the trees and bushes which alone gave them audience.

'I met Sue in the third year of my course in London.' Khumbo began his long story, turning round to face

Grace in the dark, and making the single bed squeak miserably.

'She turned out to be a nice girl and soon we discovered we had much in common in addition to our course. So we moved out of the hostel and rented a room. For the rest of my stay we lived together.'

'Like man and wife?' she asked, instinctively rolling away from him. Khumbo immediately lost the warmth he had been enjoying from Grace's body. She nearly rolled over, but Khumbo pulled her back.

'Yes, you might say like man and wife.'

'And you say she is not your wife?'

'Well, we are not married yet,' Khumbo attempted an explanation.

'It just doesn't make sense to me,' she said despondently.

'Let's just drop the subject,' he suggested, squeezing her against his body.

'I am not offended,' she protested. 'I am just trying to follow. That's all.'

He lay quiet, and dozed off later. When he woke he looked at his watch, which registered one o'clock. He had slept for an hour. He could not sleep again after that, mainly due to the size of the bed which made it impossible for him to relax in his sleep. He was amazed at the way Grace slept, letting the purring from her nostrils fill the silent night. He, on his part, let his mind wander across miles, and even galaxies, reaching out to his maker's role in the events that now engulfed his life.

He rolled out of bed at four, intending to spend the next two to three hours in his own, but his head weighed a ton and he ended up knocking pots and plates all over the place. This earned him a shout of disapproval from Grace.

'Who's that?' she screamed.

'Shsh,' he whispered, but loudly enough to be heard in the next room.

'What are you doing there stalking around like a thief?'

'I have to go,' he said.

'What time is it?'

'Four o'clock.'

'Come back into bed,' she commanded. 'It won't be light for another one-and-a-half hours or so.'

He stumbled his way back and in his effort to avoid the plates and pots he found himself hitting some solid, soundless object. His toes burned, and he cursed himself.

'Stop being a baby and get back into bed,' she coaxed.

When he got back inside the blanket it took him another twenty minutes to forget the toes and respond to Grace's advances. It was only afterwards that he slept again.

She shook him violently.

'Listen, Khumbo,' she was saying to him in his half-awake state. 'People are already going about their work. You better go.'

'Huh!' he grunted, his head cracking groundnut shells.

'You had better go, now.'

'What time is it?'

'Six o'clock. C'mon,' she insisted.

He was up and dressed in minutes at the mention of the time.

'Bye,' he said, hurriedly smacking a kiss on her cheek. 'Thanks for a wonderful night.'

'Thanks for what?'

He didn't answer, and was already reaching for the door.

'Your jacket!' she shouted to him, now enjoying the last part of the drama.

'Oh, thanks,' he said, snatching it away.

'The scandal... oh, the scandal,' she kept saying to herself.

He didn't stop to consider the immediacy of Grace's statement, and went ahead to open the door. He immediately stepped back into the room with the speed of a mouse at the meow of a cat.

'What is it now?' Grace enquired, more amused than angry.

'Why didn't you wake me up earlier?'

'I've been doing just that for the past hour,' she explained. 'I might as well have been shaking a barren mango tree.'

'You should have let me go when I wanted to.'

'Now you have to blame me,' she protested as she disappeared into the bedroom. Then she called, 'You better come in here. At this time these women can just walk in looking for salt or some such silly thing.'

He entered the bedroom he had vacated minutes earlier.

'Should anything go wrong – I mean very wrong – jump into bed and I'll tell them I have a sick relation here,' she explained.

'Nobody comes into the room?' he enquired anxiously.

'Well, it's usually at my invitation or encouragement.'

'When is it safe to go out?'

'I'll leave you here when I go to school. Lock the door and wait until around nine. Then you can creep out.'

'What will the women be doing then?' he asked.

'They will have got rid of their husbands and school children. Which means getting together for morning gossip. If you walk out then, you will just provide them with a menu for the morning feast.'

'You think it's funny, don't you?'

'I wish I could see it differently, my dear Khumbo,' she said laughing, the lips thinned to a curve, as she walked out of the bedroom, having finished tidying up the bed.

'If I were you, I would go back to bed and wait for nine o'clock in a sweet dream. By the way, if you are hungry, there is some tea in the teapot on the table. Frankly, I wish your presence here would leak out to your father. Then I would enjoy seeing you face to face with the district commissioner. Boy! that would be some scene.'

Khumbo didn't regard his situation as funny. The mention of his father changed his mind about going out early. He would indeed wait until it was gossip time, then he would peep through the torn curtain to establish the venue of the women's seminar.

'How about the key?' he asked.

'Bring it to your friend Pempho. Is there anything he doesn't know?' she asked naughtily.

It wasn't until after ten that he considered it safe to come out of the house.

Chapter Five

Billy parked his Golf between the muffler tinsmith and the building which housed Vubi and Company, legal practitioners and commissioners of oaths, etc. He managed to squeeze in due to the size of the car. Even then he had difficulty forcing his way out through the half-open door. The sawmill behind the buildings gave him protection against encroachment from the backyard. Having pulled himself out, he quickly looked ahead and past the hedge in front of the building, his eyes scurrying across, back and forth, and sideways just to establish if there was any danger in proceeding into the office. It was as if every branch on trees had grown eyes.

Once inside, he went straight to the point.

'I think I am in trouble,' he said as he pulled out a chair from under the desk.

'Sit down,' Mr Vubi said with a smile. 'And tell me all about it.'

Mr Vubi's confidence always had a clinical touch. He went for a file on the shelf and walked back slowly while flipping through it.

'I think I am being watched,' Billy said before Mr Vubi sat down.

'Oh dear.' Mr Vubi remained standing. 'And what for?'

'You see,' Billy paused, somewhat embarrassed by what he had to tell. Mr Vubi stared at him and remained quiet.

'They came to search my house.'

'When?'

'Last night.'

'What were they looking for? What did they take?'

'I wasn't there.'

'You mean they broke into your house?'

'Yes. They tore the place apart – mattresses, suitcases. They left such a mess.'

'Have you noticed anything missing?' Mr Vubi leaned on the table as Billy hesitated.

'Mr Dala, you must tell me everything,' he said as he repositioned his drooping spectacles.

Billy felt as if he was being questioned by a doctor about some communicable disease he had contracted but whose name he couldn't pronounce.

'Well, my curios.'

'They took curios?'

Billy nodded.

Mr Vubi sat down and started taking notes. When Billy looked up, their eyes met, Mr Vubi's peering above the rims of the spectacles.

'You are not telling me everything, Mr Dala,' Mr Vubi

said looking at him fiercely. 'Now let me warn you. I have heard about curios from elsewhere. There is talk of some major Indian hemp catch. Now if you are associated with it, however remotely, I must know. Because if it's the same story, some big shots are involved. Right?'

Billy nodded.

'Some big shots are involved,' Mr Vubi repeated, his stare dampening Billy's otherwise strong resolve to stand up to him.

Billy stared back, this time meekly, this time seemingly on the receiving end of whatever verbal punishment might ensue. Well, he was thinking to himself, tell me what to do. You are my lawyer.

'I want to know everything,' he said, with an emphasis on the last word which left Billy in no doubt about his lawyer's 'either deliver or else' attitude.

'It's hemp,' Billy said and offered no more. He had learnt to volunteer only what was necessary. His beard, as was usual in time of intense emotional stress, was the victim of his discomfiture.

'How much?'

'A lot.'

'How much?' Mr Vubi was getting impatient, transparently so.

'This time, not less than K50,000 worth.'

'You mean there are other times?'

'Yes.'

'How many?' Oh, this man won't let go! One thing

he didn't like about Mr Vubi – his bullying tactics. You would think he was working for the prosecution.

'I can't remember.'

'You've got to remember,' he screamed. 'Good heavens, you must remember. If what I'm hearing is true, you've got to remember.'

'What have you heard?' Billy was now caught unawares.

Tactics or no tactics, if this man was his lawyer it was time he showed where his loyalty was.

'Don't mind what I've heard.' Mr Vubi now stood up. 'If they decide to go to court it's your word against theirs.'

'What do you mean if they decide to go to court?' Billy asked, also standing up.

Mr Vubi's secretary entered, carrying a tray with two cups of tea and a bowl of sugar. They hadn't even heard her knock. Billy sat down again, leaving his lawyer to maintain his domineering position. In his subdued position Billy went for his beard like one possessed, ensuring that each time he looked at his palms he had a strand or two to throw away. His eyes were blazing, not necessarily at Mr Vubi, who now symbolised the object of the fury in his eyes, but at the real enemy, the eventual victims when he laid his hands on them. He had served them well, like hell he had. And now that he was telling it all, he had no way of knowing how far the repercussions would go. But now he had resolved to fight with one objective, the security of his mother and wife and the sanctity of his unborn child. No matter what happened to him, his family must never regret the moment he made the decision to fight. They must never live to curse the day he weighed *them* on the scale and found *them* wanting. They must live to bless the helplessness that had reduced him to one of *them* by succumbing to the selling of his soul for thirty pieces of silver.

'I don't smoke the stuff,' Billy started now that he had calmed down somewhat. 'But when I was approached to consider using my farm…'

'Your farm? What farm?'

'Well, it's my mother's really. It's just that I assist her in managing it.' He took a sip of tea.

'Well, so I was offered a good down payment, lots of money. I didn't turn it down. I used it. I needed money to get my Renault back on the road. I did and couldn't pay it back any other way.'

And so the story went on and on… When he stood up to go, Mr Vubi saw him to the door and patted him on the shoulder.

'If it goes to court, we are lucky…'

'You keep saying if… What stops them now that they have evidence?'

'Leave it to me. The most we can do is prevent them using you as a scapegoat. There are lots of big fish in the net and it's beginning to look dirty.'

As Billy walked out into the sun, he did not care any more how many eyes were on the branches, or how many ears on the tree trunks. He walked steadily on towards his Golf. And for the first time he felt very proud of his acquisition.

But most of all, he felt proud that what had started as a misfortune had actually turned into a blessed opportunity for him to purify his soul as he declared his 'sins' openly and denounced those who had smeared his name and that of the likes of him – so innocent and usually naive, all for survival in these most difficult times. He would fight them in the open and purge himself of the guilt.

He revved his Golf with all the might that his big foot could unleash and enjoyed the smoke and the noise as he reversed from his parked position.

Without much prompting Khumbo found himself extending his visit in Nkhotakota for an afternoon, a day, days, until he couldn't count the days any more. His interest in Grace grew in spite of his otherwise gloomy corner. Baba surprisingly allowed him a fair degree of latitude in regard to his relationship with Pempho and Grace. As for the latter, Baba's tolerance had much to do with her being a more palatable alternative to the much-talked-about Sue. Khumbo was quite happy to enjoy his return and the little town had offered the quiet and peace of mind he hadn't known in Lilongwe. Consequently, he kept postponing his trip to his mother's motel.

Late one night he was surprised to see the lantern in his father's room still on in addition to that in the sitting-room. He proceeded as noiselessly as he had done on many occasions before, this time in the hope that his father had forgotten to put out the light. When he tried the key he discovered that the door was unlocked. He pushed it open. Sitting in his favourite chair was Sam, fast asleep, his mouth wide open. His father walked in from his bedroom.

'We have been waiting for you,' Baba said, still standing.

'Anything wrong?' Khumbo asked.

'You better hear it from him,' Baba said, his head turning in Sam's direction.

Sam was now awake and busy wiping his mouth with his shirt sleeve. They shook hands.

'Anything wrong, Sam?' Khumbo wasted no time.

'It's Billy,' Sam said.

Khumbo looked at him and then at Baba without saying anything.

'He has been picked up,' Sam said.

Khumbo walked the extra two yards to an empty chair and sat down heavily. He continued looking at Sam for some time while feeling Baba's eyes on him all the time. Looking at Baba's bony face and grey head Khumbo remembered the persistent and unanswered question, 'Where did I go wrong?'

'You better go back and sort this out,' Baba said, as if in a trance.

'What exactly is wrong?' Khumbo said at last.

'Drugs,' Sam said resignedly.

Khumbo was silent for a while.

'Drugs?' Khumbo asked without expecting an answer.

'Well,' Sam interrupted. 'And illegal importation of vehicles.'

'But...' Khumbo paused as if suddenly lightning had struck and in a flash everything around him had been laid bare and exposed. Billy's nakedness was even more pronounced in the exposure.

'The curios, of course!' he cried.

'It's the South African connection,' Sam said. Then he stood up. 'He'll need a lawyer fast.'

'I don't know any lawyer,' Khumbo said.

'He has one,' Sam offered. 'But Billy is already talking too much. Big names are involved. And that's dangerous.'

Baba withdrew to his bedroom without a word. Khumbo watched him close the door and the good night he felt like shouting across past the closed door rolled into a lump in his throat.

'Come with me,' Khumbo said after recovering his voice. 'We'll share my room.'

As soon as they were in the bedroom, Sam felt for his breast pocket and fished out several letters, all but one from London, the exception being 'On Government Service'. He started with Sue's. Most of the letters carried the same message about her missing him. She wrote weekly.

The khaki envelope contained his biggest surprise. It was with much pleasure that the Malawi Government was offering Dr Khumbo Dala the post of a Medical Officer within the Public Service. He was being offered a basic salary at the bottom of professional category A. His probation would be for two years (twenty-four months), at the end of which, if successful, his salary would be revised accordingly. He would be advised of the station to which he was being posted as soon as the enclosed agreement had been signed and returned to the Training Office. For further information regarding the appointment he was being referred to the *Public Service Regulations*.

Khumbo's reaction to the correspondence was total confusion. Letters from Sue would ordinarily brighten his spirits, that from the Public Service Commission would give him immense satisfaction. But now he had to examine his situation afresh. Sam's attempt to keep a conversation going was a dismal failure.

'There's something else,' Sam said, now lying in his bed facing the roof. It took Khumbo some time to realise that Sam was changing the subject.

'I've been meaning to tell you about Billy and Chimwemwe.'

'Which Chimwemwe?' Khumbo asked from his lying position.

'Musa,' Sam said.

'What about them?'

'They are married, you know,' Sam was still looking at the roof, following the beams, rafters, etc., as they crisscrossed to create an impressive pattern. Modern houses wouldn't show beams or rafters. All one has to look at are square or rectangular shapes on the ceiling. At the same time he could feel Khumbo's eyes on him, boring their way through Sam's skin. But Sam had now learnt not to look at angry eyes head-on.

Khumbo eyed him like a mamba whose tail has been chopped off but whose bleeding has not killed it yet: only made it more vengeful and dangerous.

'I've tried to tell you before,' pleaded Sam, sensing the silent angry eyes across the room. A gecko fell from the roof with a smack which gave both of them a start.

'Actually,' Sam explained, 'they have been living together for a long time.'

Khumbo rose from the bed, letting the letters scatter around his feet, and walked out into the *khonde*. The sky was suddenly empty in its brightness and the night around him weighed heavily on him with a nothingness he could not explain. Billy's choice in life, it seemed, had been to hurt those he held dearest. Chimwemwe had been his childhood sweetheart and for some years he wrote from London. After Sue he had stopped writing…

October, eight years earlier, he had embarked on an adventurous study tour at the age of twenty. Chimwemwe could not come all the way from Nkhotakata to see him off for fear of raising her parents' suspicions. His mother had remained behind on account of funds; this actually saved Khumbo the embarrassment of having to say farewell to his mother in tears. She had cried enough at home. And now, the parting scene eight years ago slowly unfolded itself, the memory of it imposing itself on his exhausted mind.

Chimwemwe, only sixteen, peeping through the window, her round fair-skinned face pleading with him to remember his promise and return to her. He remembered her athletic stature, and how her legs would carry her across the football field to claim the first position in any race, her blossoming bust exuding a pride which left Khumbo's heart melting inside him. She could have captained the school's netball team if it weren't, at least that was everyone's belief, for the predominance of Christians on the staff which did not give Moslem children much chance to excel. His mother, Mai Nabanda, stood on the verandah and let her tears flow freely, muttering the only words he would remember for a long time:

'Who will take care of my young man? Who will?'

In school Billy had shared desks with Chimwemwe and that's how Khumbo's relationship with her started, with Billy faithfully delivering letters and messages. But the girl had proved too clever in class for Billy. She had passed her Primary School Leaving Certificate Examinations but could not proceed to secondary school as her father considered the education already acquired enough for a girl if she was to remain subservient to her husband.

On the day he left for the UK, Billy, Baba, and Khumbo sat on the balcony and listened to the whines of the VC10, watched the engineers, groundsmen, and ground hostesses scurrying to and from the plane. Billy could not wait for his turn to attract so much attention in the little town of Nkhotakota with all the girls saying flattering things about a local hero. And now, as he waited for Khumbo to leave the surface of the earth and head for the clouds, he thought his time would come – had to come.

'You are sure it's seven years,' enquired Baba anxiously.

'Yes, Baba, plus one or two,' answered Khumbo. 'You can't do medicine in less time.'

'You will be a big man when you come back, a doctor,' Baba started later along the same dreamy vein. 'All those years without a wife to support you?'

Khumbo thought he was not obliged to reply.

'You cannot come for a while to find yourself a wife?'

'No, I cannot,' Khumbo left no room for further speculation.

'Still, I think it's improper,' he persisted, 'if I can be of assistance, do write.'

'Baba,' Khumbo pleaded. 'I can't waste time thinking about a wife and expect to do well in my studies.'

That simple reasoning seemed to work magic on Baba who now just looked fixedly at the big aeroplane. Before he could formulate a response, the announcement came, just in time to stifle whatever final remarks Baba had deemed appropriate for this occasion. Khumbo jumped to his feet, shook Billy's hand and then Baba's, deaf to all their mutterings, but not blind to the moistening eyes.

He ascended the steps into the lounge, and disappeared between two immigration officers manning the passage to the waiting-room.

He then reflected on the instances when he had received very informative letters from home. Baba's first letter was all ecstasy:

> My beloved son,
> I am writing to share with you the good news of your brother's success. He has done so well that he has been selected to attend Blantyre Secondary School. The whole town is talking, not just about Billy, but also about you, the whole family...

And so he went on to remind him of his responsibility, family pride, and what a good example he had been. Then, much later, he wrote again, addressing him in the same manner:

> I have just come across a most disturbing piece of news concerning you and Chimwemwe Musa. I cannot believe that my son, for whom I have sacrificed so much to bring up in the Christian fold, can go out in search of a Moslem for a life partner. I always ask myself: Where did I go wrong? What have I done to deserve this ingratitude?

Khumbo had been angered by his father's intrusion into his private life and, as a result, his communication home had become less frequent as time went on. Letters from

Chimwemwe also piled up, unanswered. In the end she gave up writing. Eventually, only Billy wrote so that in his last year or so in London he had hardly heard anything about his family or Chimwemwe. Billy's letters had of late concentrated on trivial matters.

Unlike Nkhotakota, Salima had changed somewhat. The construction of the lakeshore road had meant the introduction of more shops while jobs offered by the contractors had afforded the male folk means of improving the living standards of their families. Coupled with this was the tourist industry which offered the town a share of its proceeds. It was, therefore, not difficult to conceive of the success which met Mr John Frederick's idea of a motel in the name of Mai Nabanda's Gona Pano Motel. There was an inscription on an arch erected in front of the building:

> Are you weary?
> Looking for comfort?
> Mai Nabanda is the answer.

Gona Pano Motel had now become Mai Nabanda's preoccupation since John Frederick's return to England. She did not allow her concentration on the business to be interfered with by the absence of a man in the house. Two mistakes in life were enough; there was no point hoping that a third man would produce miracles. The motel was itself a miracle. The story might have been different had John turned out a selfish and uncompromising chauvinist, but he had provided for his son in a manner that also provided for Mai Nabanda. Indeed, John's provision for her had provided a base for a flourishing business. And now Billy was in trouble. That was more important than anything else now. She had to find out what kind of trouble.

She put the receiver down and threw herself into the sofa next to the telephone. Sam had been brief about Billy's arrest. She would have to leave immediately. But two problems compounded her dilemma. What would Chimwemwe's reaction be? Sam asked for Khumbo who had left Lilongwe to visit his parents. It was weeks since he left. Did he... indeed could he have preferred his father to her? Well, Khumbo had always been Baba's favourite. But...

'Mother,' Mai Nabanda was startled by Chimwemwe's voice. 'Are you all right?'

'Hm? Yes,' Mai Nabanda mumbled. 'It's the telephone call,' Mai Nabanda answered, trying to regain her composure.

'I see,' Chimwemwe said, leaving it to her elder to take her time or even choose whether to divulge the contents of the conversation or not.

'It's Billy,' Mai Nabanda said at last.

'What about Billy, mother?' she said restlessly. 'You must tell me, mother.'

'He's been arrested.'

'Nooo, not my husband,' Chimwemwe moaned as she rushed to her bedroom. Mai Nabanda had to forget her weakness and rush to contain her daughter-in-law. 'I warned you mother. This *chamba* business will only bring trouble.'

Mai Nabanda burst into the room before the door could slam closed and sat by Chimwemwe's bed. She watched the young woman struggle on the bed and wondered which of the two caused Chimwemwe greater pain: Billy's arrest or his child inside her. When she had sobbed herself quiet, Chimwemwe sat up and leaned against the wall, her legs spread out as if not caring who might be at the other end.

'I am going to Lilongwe,' Chimwemwe declared and Mai Nabanda knew there was no stopping her.

'I know, and I am coming too,' Mai Nabanda replied.

'I am going – now.'

'My daughter,' Mai Nabanda tried to be firm with her. 'What about Khumbo?'

'I am not interested in Khumbo,' she almost shrieked.

'Yes, I know,' said the older woman calmly. 'But the arrangement was that we would talk to Khumbo first. That would make it easier on both of you.'

'On him you mean…'

'Okay, on him. But…'

'Mother,' Chimwemwe interrupted. 'Khumbo broke his promise and I cannot be blamed for that. I am going. Now.'

Chimwemwe leapt off the bed and went for her suitcase.

'I know, I know. It was his fault. But can't you see that you are still in the same house?'

'So?' Chimwemwe asked, on the brink of tears again. 'What was I to do? It's my fault. Let me handle it my way. Right now my husband is in prison and he needs me. If you want to worry about Khumbo, go ahead. He is your son, not mine.' With that she went into the wardrobe like one possessed.

'You have always been strongheaded, my daughter,' Mai Nabanda said as she left the room for her own. 'I was only trying to help. We'll all look stupid when Khumbo starts firing questions. And I have never known him to run short of questions.'

They were ready to leave inside an hour, making sure the pick-up was loaded with everything they would need in the city: blankets, firewood, charcoal, beans, flour, and some kitchen utensils. She knew her son so well that she even carried salt and sugar. In any case, no sane mother, aunt, sister, or grandmother left to visit her relation in town without sufficient food provisions, since it was generally accepted that living in town was tantamount to starving. Any villager took it upon herself or himself to provide for the town dweller. If the town dweller decided to lavish on them in return – soap, sugar, clothes, etc. – let that be according to their conscience. Otherwise such gifts were bought in the spirit of give alone, not give and take.

After making arrangements with her staff on how to

run the motel in her absence, she, Chimwemwe, and George John Fredrick, her coloured son, left for the city.

By the time Khumbo applied the brakes behind the Datsun pick-up, two things had already been established. He had already spotted the familiar, tall figure of his mother. Second, he inferred from this that Chimwemwe must be around. His mind was now thrown into a whirlwind and he immediately regretted Baba's decision to join him that morning. He now cursed himself for letting his father change his mind.

'Billy is my son,' Baba had said decisively that morning. 'And I will come.'

Khumbo had let him dictate again and now he had to deal with whatever confrontation might arise from this gathering. He was so lost in his confusion he did not see the owner of the shadow behind him. It was Mai Nabanda. Further down, Chimwemwe stood next to the house inspecting the scene by the car.

'Come inside, Chimwemwe,' Mai Nabanda said as she led her daughter-in-law by the hand, even before she had talked to her son. Chimwemwe followed, albeit reluctantly. Her body was being dragged from the scene.

Mai Nabanda came back and asked Khumbo out of the car, and performed the same task of leading him into the house. Much to his relief, Chimwemwe was not in the room when Khumbo and Mai Nabanda entered. Khumbo sat down while his mother proceeded to the kitchen. In a flash, he saw Chimwemwe's image, her belly protruding with the pride of imminent motherhood. The athlete and netball player he had left behind in a second-hand satin dress bought outside an Indian shop, the kinky uncombed hair, and the dusty bare feet, all these had given way to a confident smile, straight hair and imported ready-made dresses. She obviously watched her weight so that her impending motherhood did not have a generally negative effect on her figure.

'*Muli bwanji Achimwene?*' his mother greeted him as she sat down beside him.

'*Ndiri bwino.*' Then after a pause he sighed and returned the greeting. '*Kaya inu muli bwanji?*' His mind was on Chimwemwe and he couldn't help feeling jealous about her carrying Billy's baby.

'*Ndiri bwino.*'

Chimwemwe walked in before the formal greetings were over; indeed before mother and son had warmed to each other and cleared up a few doubts about each other. Mai Nabanda was at a loss as to whether to send Chimwemwe back into her room or not. It was in fact Chimwemwe who was to make that decision for her. It was the same Chimwemwe who had decided to challenge her father and religion to marry Billy. It was the same Chimwemwe who had in spite of this challenge to her religion and parents made the decision not to compromise her religious beliefs and values and had, therefore, refused to become Christian, refused to be wedded in church and had as a result resorted to a *khonde* wedding – a simple but truly traditional officiation involving the agreement between the *ankhoswe* to let the 'children' marry. An exchange of chicken and gifts and the couple were man and wife. A huge feast followed and in no time at all the Moslems and Christians were eating together, each making the most of the occasion. Only one face was missed on that day – well, two faces really – which would have made her victory and enjoyment total: Baba and Khumbo.

'How is my *mlamu*?' Chimwemwe addressed Khumbo from the door arms akimbo. Khumbo's mouth gaped wide open and deep furrows cut into his forehead.

'Yes, it's me, *mlamu*.' She walked several steps and offered her hand, which he shook perfunctorily. 'Welcome back!'

The two women in the room with Khumbo had one thing in common: they both dwarfed him, and a lot of men at that, both physically and mentally. They operated with such confidence you wondered how much more a man had to fight to regain dominance.

Mai Nabanda grabbed Chimwemwe by the wrist and walked her back to her room. By the time they reached the door Chimwemwe had broken down and the sobbing was as clear as the *timba* chirping on a quiet morning. Khumbo also wiped a tear with his palm.

Back in the car, Sam's discomfiture was total. He had sworn to be absent when Chimwemwe and Khumbo met;

but here he was, again overtaken by events. He and Baba remained in the car, both of them hit by the significance of Mai Nabanda's and Chimwemwe's presence here, but each viewing the situation from a different standpoint. He knew enough of the family history to suggest what course of action to take.

He opened his front passenger door and came out to open the back door.

'Come with me, Baba,' Sam called out to Baba who was jolted from his confusion.

'What… What did you say?' Baba asked.

'Come with me. My house is the next one. I think you'll be better off with me.'

'Of course, of course,' he said as he stepped out, his stick going before him. 'My bag is in the boot.'

Sam tried to open the boot and found it locked. 'I will collect it later,' he said as he led the old man away.

By evening the arrangements had been completed. Khumbo and Baba would both be accommodated in Sam's house, all the womenfolk put up at Billy's. Most of that evening was spent discussing the implications of a newspaper article.

> BIG NAMES IN DRUGS SCANDAL
>
> At the first hearing of a drug and *chamba* case being held in the Magistrates' Court in Lilongwe yesterday, Mr Billy Dala pleaded not guilty to the charge of being in possession of

mandrax and Indian hemp and not guilty to that of trading in *mandrax* and Indian hemp.

Speaking on behalf of the defendant, the defence counsel sought clearance to call into the witness box a very prominent police official. The defence case rested on Mr Dala's role as a go-between between the top official and the buyers.

At this point both the prosecution and defence counsel were called to the bench for consultation following which the hearing was adjourned to a date to be decided later.

This case has raised much speculation as to who the big name would turn out to be. Names are already being tossed about in drinking places and observers are anxious to see justice done. The question being asked is: How can we as a nation effectively fight drug abuse, *chamba*-smoking and corruption if the name and level of the law-breaker are allowed to influence court decisions? We hope the law will be allowed to take its course.

Mr Billy Dala is a Personnel Officer in the Civil Service. At about 11.45pm, 16th October, Mr Dala was arrested in his house having admitted ownership of four curios all in the shape of our local cartoon trickstar, Zuze. Three of these contained Indian hemp locally grown and processed, the fourth mandrax. These had been collected from the house earlier, in his absence, a point which is likely to strengthen the defence case.

Grace stormed into Pempho's office without knocking.

'He's gone, eh? Just like that?' she cried.

'No, no, no! He left you a note,' Pempho said as he handed her a note.

'A note,' she snarled as she grabbed the note, tore it to pieces without reading it, and threw the pieces out of the window. 'Have I suddenly become a leper that he can't touch? Have I?'

'Miss Ndele, please, there are school children out there…'

'So?'

'Let me explain,' he pleaded as he forced her on to a chair.

'There is a problem he has to sort out. A family problem.'

'His mother I bet…'

'No. His brother…'

'I don't believe it. Too convenient.'

'Well, his brother Billy has been picked up.'

'What?' she sneered, her lips releasing a sharp derogatory sucking noise that sounded like she was blowing into a muffled whistle.

'That's what he has to find out.'

'Then why do I have to hear it from you?' she asked as she regretfully eyed the pieces of what had contained her special message. 'Do you know what he said in the letter?'

'No, I'm sorry.'

Her eyes blazed as it dawned on her that it was futile to try to reconstruct the tiny pieces of paper now littering the grounds outside the headmaster's office. The fury was exacerbated by the suspicion that Khumbo was on the verge of saying something serious to her, that the few weeks they had spent together had melted him into a warm, lovable, and serious mate. Of course she needed time to get a committed statement from him. Of course she had to pretend that the seriousness of his relationship with Sue deserved some respect. Of course she had to play up her relationship with Dan Kapala in Blantyre as a way of keeping him hanging on.

But now all those expectations had failed the final test. By not being there to hear Khumbo's last words when leaving town, she had been denied the opportunity to solicit some sign from him on which to pin her hopes. Or was the manner of his departure itself the very statement she needed to put herself in the right perspective? As she walked out of the office without saying goodbye, she knew that she would never know what Khumbo had put on paper. She only wondered, how do you remind a man where you think he left off when you next meet him?

Chapter Six

Khumbo and Baba walked past the sign announcing the existence of a legal practice under the name Vubi and Company, legal practitioners, commissioners of oaths, etc. They headed for the reception desk and stated their intentions even before they were invited to do so. The receptionist referred them to the secretary and the latter guided them into the inner room.

'Do come in, please,' the boss said. 'I am Mr Vubi, and you must be Dr Dala.'

'Yes, I am. How do you do?'

'And you must be Mr Dala, the father?'

'Yes, sir,' said Baba with a firmness that left them in no doubt as to who was the eldest in the group.

Mr Vubi beckoned Khumbo to come alone into the office in spite of Baba's displeasure.

'I must see you alone,' Mr Vubi said.

The secretary offered Baba a chair after she had closed the door and then sat in her swivel chair facing the busy traffic on the road. Within the few minutes they had been there, Khumbo had mastered the details of the congested offices. Five chairs in the cubicle of a reception, a corridor, an adjoining office leading to Mr Vubi's office whose walls were lined with shelves filled with files and legal volumes.

Khumbo sat opposite Mr Vubi and waited patiently while the lawyer sorted out his papers.

'Now, we've to start at the beginning,' Mr Vubi said.

'Which is…?' Khumbo said conversationally.

'Your brother's problem is difficult. But he is not helping himself by behaving the way he is doing.'

'How is be behaving?' Khumbo asked. 'He has pleaded not guilty, hasn't he?' Khumbo asked, trying to clear the fuzziness in his head. 'How else is he supposed to behave?'

'No, no, no, not that,' Mr Vubi interjected. 'I'll explain.' And then he went for another file on the shelf. Khumbo in the meantime loosened his tie and the top button of his shirt.

'Billy's problem is that he is wounded – morally I mean – and suspects, and he may be right, that he has been sacrificed by certain top men in order to cover up their tracks in the muddy business.'

'I remember reading that in the paper.'

'No, you didn't read that in the paper. You just got hints. What you were supposed to read never came through.'

'You mean there has been intervention…?' Khumbo asked.

'That's the only explanation.'

Khumbo rose from his chair and walked towards the only window in the office.

'There may never be a trial…' Mr Vubi went on to explain.

'You mean they will release him?'

'No.' Mr Vubi shook his head.

'They cannot just keep him locked up when they can't prove his guilt,' Khumbo protested impotently.

'They can prove his guilt all right,' Mr Vubi replied. 'But not in court. We can negotiate his release. To do that we need his co-operation. Six months, a year at most.'

'Mr Vubi, that just cripples his career.'

'Billy doesn't need his job,' Mr Vubi said.

'What are you talking about?' Khumbo asked, now totally perplexed.

'You don't seem to understand. Billy doesn't need to work. In this business, it doesn't take one long to accumulate money.'

'You don't mean that boy has been driving that rotten car…'

'Out of choice. You see if he lived in the style of his choice, they would have caught up with him long ago. Have you been to your mother's motel?'

'No, not yet.'

'That enterprise is now a joint business. You mother is such an enterprising woman she has expanded what was just a motel into farming and transport. And Billy is a major shareholder in that.' He paused to answer a call which the receptionist described as urgent.

Khumbo used the occasion to reappraise his family

position. Mai Nabanda looked prosperous enough, if the brand new Datsun pick-up was anything to go by. Both she and Chimwemwe wore expensive imported clothes. But not Billy. Everything about Billy confirmed his declared poverty, misery, and victimisation by a socio-economic system he had become a part of through fate only. It was bad enough to be told that Billy controlled a lucrative drug trade but that he was the brains behind a successful motel-cum-transport-farming business was to be asked to stretch his imagination too far. At the same time he had no reason to doubt the bespectacled, balding, middle-aged lawyer on the phone, always making a point firmly without losing his persuasive smile. He must be around thirty-five. But he seemed to know enough about Billy's affairs.

'If what you have just said is true,' Khumbo resumed after Mr Vubi had replaced the receiver, 'Billy could be in for a long time.'

'That's right,' Mr Vubi said. 'But that's where negotiations outside the court come in. A nominal sentence leading to six months or slightly more – just to silence critics, you see what I mean.'

'It's up to Billy, really,' Khumbo said, rather defeated. 'Any chance of bail?'

'No. But you must help him make up his mind,' Mr Vubi said. 'I have offered my professional help, but he seems set on a suicidal course and keeps demanding a trial. Not many people would like to see him free until assurances have been made.'

'What exactly have they against him? Just the *chamba* in the curios?'

'Listen to this, Dr Dala,' Mr Vubi said. 'He has agreed that the two-acre tobacco farm next to Gona Pano Motel is his. That farm generates half-a-million-dollar business a year – US dollars, not Kwacha. There are three South African truck drivers who have made sworn statements that the mandrax and *chamba* in their possession at the time of their arrest at the border were supplied by him. They have left out a few details to save his neck – like the car they brought him. Now if he goes on trial, he must consider his family – his wife and mother. They are the ones managing the business. They stand to lose everything.'

'You mean Billy doesn't see all that?' Khumbo asked.

'I can't understand him. That's why I need you. He has this thing about bringing somebody down from towers of authority. That's the only thing that will give him satisfaction.'

'I will have to try,' Khumbo said as he rose to go.

'Whatever you tell your father, I wouldn't tell him about your mother if I were you,' Mr Vubi said as he saw him to the door.

Khumbo walked out without uttering another word. Mr Vubi's presumptions about the Dala family disgusted him thoroughly. Baba followed him just as quietly. Khumbo started the car and off they went.

'Your mother must be behind all this,' Baba said, much to Khumbo's amazement.

Khumbo turned to face Baba and said nothing, but marvelled at the unflinching prophetic stature of his ageing father.

'Your mother always had this big hunger for wealth, for big position. She never was the woman to be satisfied with a man's efforts to provide for her. Now she has passed that on to the children.'

Khumbo drove on in silence, now reflecting on Mr Vubi's revelations. He parked the car behind Sam's house and let Baba proceed into the house while he walked across the yard to see his mother.

Mai Nabanda was big, tall, and light in complexion, but she carried her weight with ease, crushing noisily anything that her big feet pounced on. Everyone concluded she had passed on these features to Billy.

'There is a telegram for you,' Mai Nabanda said to Khumbo as he sat down in what had become his favourite chair. She went into the bedroom to collect it, her trunk vibrating with her quick movements.

Khumbo had become used to seeing Chimwemwe walking out of Billy's room and going about as any wife would do. He had now reconciled himself to the fact that his one-time girlfriend was now his sister-in-law, although he couldn't get used to the sarcastic tone in Chimwemwe's voice every time she called him *mlamu*.

He would never stop marvelling at her transformation, which condemned his weakness even more: he had used his father's intervention to break with his childhood ties, and Billy, for whatever reason, had picked up where he left off with or without Baba's blessing. At least he had the strength to act like a man where Khumbo himself had failed.

Now he was looking at an alliance between Chimwemwe and Mai Nabanda, both of whom had their docility transformed into enterprising acumen, the level of which would have been unimaginable ten years ago. Mai Nabanda brought the telegram which read simply:

Meet me at the airport on Saturday
Flight No. BA 052, 9am local time
Sue

'It's best that Chimwemwe doesn't know about it,' his mother said, half-whispering.

'Why not?' Khumbo said, almost screaming.

'Quietly. She is in the bedroom.'

'Mother,' Khumbo said, back to his normal voice. 'There can never be anything.'

'You are my child, *achimwene*,' Mai Nabanda said calmly. 'And I am a woman also. Things like these can hurt for a long time.'

Khumbo could have said nonsense – *zopusa zimenezo* – but this was not England. His mother's views or advice had to be respected and therefore could not be dismissed in any manner, derogatory or otherwise. Displeasure was all the emotion he could express and, even then, not verbally but only through the wrinkles on his forehead.

'I guess you have been to see the lawyer,' she said in a question that sounded flat enough to pass for a statement.

'Hm,' he grunted, nodding his head, his forehead furrowing more and more.

'Then you know the story,' she continued in the same vein. He looked at her hard.

'I know, mother,' he said in a tired voice. 'His story.'

'It's the same story, my son,' she concluded.

'Then why?'

'You are asking why, *achimwene*,' she said. 'I never associated you with that question before. By not asking it, you avoided the wrath of your father. Was it not always Billy who saw the need to ask why? And what did he get in return? Punishment on everybody's behalf.'

She paused as her mind was driven back years to the boys' childhood. She was breathing heavily, as she always did in moments of intense emotion. The marks Baba's belt left on Billy's back reappeared in their rawness, and yet all she could do at the time was withdraw into the kitchen corner and cry silently, for any attempt to check Baba in his fury was tantamount to a plea of guilt in a murder case.

'No, my son,' she resumed her monologue. 'Your *why* is years too late. The pot has already been broken. And you tell me now if you can put the pieces together.'

'You don't seem to regret it,' he said, his voice surprisingly calmer than the storm he was battling with inside him.

'Regret?' she said, now looking him straight in the eye, her chest heaving rhythmically as she mopped the sweat on her forehead with her *chitenje*. 'What do you know about regret? All my life has been one long story of regret.' She stopped to wipe a tear and blow her nose. 'My son, you are my eldest and there are still a lot of things you don't know about our family.'

Khumbo waited for more surprises, powerless to control their effect on his mind. His hand automatically went up to scratch his head. The furrowing of the forehead no longer signified anger with Mai Nabanda, but his loss of direction. He had never handled his mother when she cried.

'I had ambition like your father, like everybody else. I wanted to be a nurse. But your father wouldn't let me. He couldn't wait and I had to quit school. For years I lived in his house and suffered every humiliation you can think of. Time came when I had to find an outlet. I just had to breathe and live again.'

She blew and wiped her nose using her *chitenje*, for the free flow of her tears didn't matter any more. Khumbo on his part envied the English boys he had known who, in situations like this, would have held her hand or hugged her to offer consolation. He had to be content with the agony the revelations inflicted on his already open wounds.

'Right now,' she continued. 'Your father has been talked to. I have been talked to. But he will not forget, he will not forgive.'

'You mean you wanted him back?' Khumbo asked, perplexed.

'Who needs the other more?'

'Look at him, *mai*,' Khumbo corrected her. 'You don't pity him? I would have done the same.'

'No, you wouldn't look at it my way, only his. But that doesn't alter the fact that he will live in poverty all his life. A man's pride, that's all it is.'

Khumbo's perplexity grew. Couldn't she see what she had done to Billy? Was this the time to brag about her escape? He remembered his father's words that very morning and wondered where his real mother was – the woman who had wiped mucus off his nose and mouth, with her saliva if it became necessary? Who was this stranger now talking as if she had to bewitch her own family to achieve success in life?'

'But mother,' he found himself saying, his politeness prevailing over everything else. 'Look what you have done to Billy.'

'He will find a way out. Your father made a real man out of him and he has been my main support.'

She said this shaking her head with the pride of a hawk whose prey is clinging securely to its claws.

'Anyway, I am going to see him,' Khumbo said standing up and giving up on her. 'Are you coming?'

'We've just been,' she said. 'They won't grant him bail.'

'So I am told.' Khumbo said. 'In that case I'll let Baba come. Do you think it's all right?'

'You ask me?' she said, shrugging her shoulders. 'What else did he come here for?'

He walked out wondering how long Baba would hang around before returning to work, now hoping that he wouldn't stay long enough to meet him – not yet anyway.

It was Khumbo's turn to stand on the balcony watching the noisy aircraft nosing down, its tyres finally screeching and smoking away. He had no idea what to expect or how to react. This was the first time he and Sue had been away from each other for such a long time. Somehow he didn't feel up to the occasion. He felt a slight tremor in his spine which ended in a chill at the tail end. He didn't wave at the aeroplane like those around him; he waited, enjoying the loneliness he had created for himself by not asking anybody to join him to go to the airport. Many came out of the aircraft, but he didn't see them. When the five-feet-four blonde appeared at the door, he was filled with the kind of joy he hadn't felt for a long time now. The navy blue dress with a sailor collar and red ribbon fluttered in the breeze to create a mirage which merged well with the tropical heat. He hadn't seen the dress before – but it looked good as it flowed down and around the slim figure of a body dying for a tan.

Waving didn't help as she could not isolate his face from the others around. So he rushed down and spent the next forty-five minutes straining his neck in an attempt to keep his head above the heads blocking his view.

Sue, on her part, went through the immigration and customs formalities like a robot, anxious to bring to an end the long waiting for the cherished embrace.

Then she saw him – as soon as she had been checked out. She abandoned her trolley and ran into his arms and squeezed herself against his hot and masculine body. She looked up expecting a kiss. He pointed a finger of caution.

'Not in public, remember?' he told her with a big laugh.

'Yes... yes,' she replied, remembering, tears of joy flowing freely, truly glad that he was there to welcome her. She remembered him telling her: 'Back home we don't kiss at all. Those of us who have learnt to, do so to please the likes of you and have to do it in private. A woman is considered base if she succumbs to a man's desires too readily and shows her emotions in public.'

'I'll make it up to you, I promise,' he whispered. They released each other and Khumbo went for the trolley, and together they pushed it out into the open.

'How was immigration?' Khumbo enquired.

'Very friendly – I am only a visitor you know.'

'Of course. Customs?'

'They didn't charge me anything for the Scotch if that's your worry.'

That wasn't Khumbo's worry. He still had his own

memories of immigration and customs. They reached the car park and he heaved the baggage into the boot. The small items were thrown on to the back seat, and they started off.

'Where is everybody?' she asked, perplexed.

'Which everybody?'

'What's happened to the big family?'

'They aren't here,' he said evasively.

'You mean they don't approve of me!'

'No, I actually stopped them coming,' he lied.

She said nothing in reply, but watched him struggling to keep the car steady.

'How is Middlesex Hospital?' Khumbo tried to focus the discussion back on Sue.

'As usual.'

'How long is the leave?'

'What leave?'

Khumbo turned to face her and momentarily forgot the road. The honk from the on-coming car came just in time for him to swerve back into his lane.

He calculatingly changed into a lower gear and then another, until he stopped at the side. He sat in the car and allowed his eyes to be deceived by the mirages on the tarmac, his mind grappling with the implications of Sue's counter-question. Could she really be coming to stay? His concentration on the mirage soon calmed his nerves, his racing blood returned to its normal pace, and his mind stopped seeing visions.

'What's wrong, Khumbo?' she asked, now concerned that she had said the wrong thing.

'Nothing,' he said desperately, wondering how fate could bring Sue into the picture at such a time as this. 'I just don't understand.'

'But what did you expect me to do?' she asked, her eyes misty. 'What was I supposed to do? I missed you, Khubo.' She always pronounced his name without the *m*.

'I am sorry,' Khumbo said, rushing out and meeting her the other side of the car.

'I am sorry,' he said again without waiting for an answer. All the while he pressed her against his body.

'I said sorry,' he pleaded. 'Did you hear me?' She nodded.

'Have you forgiven me?'

She nodded again.

'Hooray! Hooray! Hooray!' cried Khumbo as he lifted her up, letting her feet leave the hot sand, and swung her around several times, for a moment forgetting the dripping sweat that had been generated first by the excitement, and now by the exercise.

She on her part responded by making herself lighter and more buoyant, meeting his lips as her legs lapped behind her, and now shedding tears of joy – the kind of joy that had been a stranger to her for a long time. He lowered her back to her feet and held her by the waist as they walked into the forest, their feet crushing the dry *gmelina* leaves. They sat down on a mound of soil and leaned against a tree.

'Am I late? It's Chiwewe, isn't it?'

Khumbo laughed, much to the surprise of both of them. Sue couldn't pronounce Chimwemwe – it was always Chiwewe.

She looked at him in total perplexity.

'I don't find it funny!' she said, her thin, pale lips distinctly Caucasian.

He laughed some more.

'I've made a fool of myself again, haven't I?' she asked, pulling herself away.

Her hair fluttered in the breeze, cutting a fine picture of a fairy in the myth of Fatsa and Nsanje, literally translated to mean Humility and Jealousy. Fatsa had been tricked by her arch-rival Nsanje, the woman with whom she shared a husband Sosa, into throwing her only son into a river in order for him to return more beautiful. Nsanje's aim was to trick Fatsa into throwing away Sosa's favourite son. When Fatsa learnt the truth she consulted the *Ng'anga* who promised to get Fatsa's son back if the younger, gullible woman obeyed her instructions to the letter. Fatsa obeyed everything the old, ugly and half-rotten woman told her to do. She was told to scratch the *Ng'anga's* worms off. She did. She was offered a meal consisting of the same worms she had scratched from the *Ng'anga's* back. She willingly joined the old woman in the meal. Fatsa was given many other tests of humility and obedience and she passed them all. The final test was to go through a fierce jungle and negotiate her way among dangerous wild animals until she found three gourds. She was to open the smallest, which she did. The baby turned out to be the most beautiful prince the village had ever seen.

He breathed gold.

His walk was majesty itself; his voice a melody from a thousand *timba*. Fatsa lived to sing praises of the *Ng'anga* all her life as she shared the glory and riches bestowed on her son, the prince.

All this flashed through Khumbo's mind as he held Sue in his arms, now squeezing her more firmly to himself.

'There is no Chimwemwe, sweetheart. There is nobody between you and me.' He felt a tinge of guilt when he remembered Grace.

She continued looking at him as he spoke, reading every gesture on his face.

And then Khumbo started laughing again. When Sue saw the genuine ecstasy on his face she caught the infectious laughter and the two rolled away like thunder on a very small island, their bodies rocking themselves into a thousand pieces of joy and pleasure.

'Can I kiss you now?' she begged.

'No, you will kiss me at the hotel. C'mon, let's go. There is so much you don't know about. I'll tell you all about it at the hotel.'

Chapter Seven

Khumbo drove through the gates after the policeman had satisfied himself with his answers on a number of security questions: Name and address? Profession? Nature of business? etc. He heard the clang of the gates as they closed behind him. As he parked the car his mind wandered from Mr Vubi to Mai Nabanda, from Sue to Baba, and then to Billy. His last visit to Billy had been brief and, unfortunately, neither of them had raised the subject of Chimwemwe. Khumbo had brought Baba who couldn't stay beyond the formal salutations. Each time he would break down and ask to be excused. As he walked back on his face would be written the agonising words, 'Where did I go wrong?'

'I'll get them,' Billy had kept saying to Khumbo.

'Look at it differently.' He snarled where he should have whispered.

'I have risked my neck while others have got rich on my account. We all knew what risks we were taking and I know who should have covered my tracks.'

'What do you mean?'

'Can't you see that they are through with me?'

Khumbo just shook his head.

'*Achimwene*,' Billy went on, 'now that my cover is blown, they won't need me any more.' He stopped pacing the floor in the small cubicle and ended up placing his big bearded head between two bars, his hair worse than Khumbo had known it before. 'It's Interpol chasing now, and they have to come out clean or you have a whole network, all the way to the top – on the line. Give me a chance to appear in court and they are all exposed.'

'But Mr Vubi thinks you could get out of this – I mean he can work out a deal…'

'What deal?' Billy snarled. 'What deal is he talking about? Somebody in there deliberately blew my cover. What is he up to? No! You, Mr Vubi, you don't understand. It's more than that. If I reveal what I know quite a number of heads would roll. Not just mine. And I'll take a few with me.' They had parted on that note.

Khumbo sat in the reception for close to half an hour before the constable returned.

'I am sorry, you can't see him today,' the constable said.

'What's wrong?'

'I don't know. Instructions.'

'What instructions?' Khumbo asked, his heart racing. 'Whose instructions?' The clang of gates throbbed in his brain as he tried to get a proper focus of events.

'Come back this afternoon,' the constable advised.

'I am not going anywhere,' Khumbo screamed. The throb was getting louder. 'I want to see your senior officer.'

'He is not available.'

'Which one?' Khumbo asked. 'How many senior officers do you have? I'll see any one of them.'

The constable shrugged his shoulders and disappeared, leaving Khumbo to mumble obscenities to himself. Then, minutes later, an officer appeared and a few stripes and the colour of his uniform betrayed his seniority.

'I am afraid Mr Dala has instructed us not to let in anybody but Mr Vubi,' the officer said.

'When did he say that?' Khumbo was now getting angry and suspicious.

'I suggest you go and get Mr Vubi before you make things worse for your brother – and yourself of course.'

'Is that a threat?' Khumbo said, pointing a finger at the officer.

'Call it what you like,' the officer said as he walked away, leaving Khumbo raving mad.

He tried to speak to a few more officers, some coming in, others going out of the building. But to no avail. He rushed out and headed for Vubi and Company.

Billy's cell door rattled as it was being unlocked. His eyes popped out as he saw the huge body fill the door. At the top of this giant was a small head. In one hand he carried a club-like stick, leaving the other hand free to hang on his waist as he stood legs astride. Billy gave up focusing on the face for details that would identify the officer whose trunk succeeded in blocking the light.

'Mr Billy Dala?' he grunted.

Billy did not answer, but instinctively lifted his hand to his forehead to create the much-needed clarity of vision.

The giant laughed.

'You don't even know your name,' the giant teased. 'And yet you claim to know us well enough to tamper with and soil the reputation of those who are doing so much for you and your type.'

He caressed the club, his attention on the club. He moved forward two steps and some light filtered through between the knock-kneed legs, the armpits, and just over the shoulders. The streak of light worsened his vision.

'A prophet is never honoured in his home,' he continued. 'How true, how true.'

'I want a fair trial…' Billy attempted to answer.

Like a flash a slap landed on Billy's bearded cheek and he reeled sideways until his hand reached for the wall to avoid hitting it.

'I didn't come to listen to you,' the officer said. 'You are the one to listen. You hear me?'

Silence. Billy had now steadied himself and the anger which he had felt upon the giant's entry had subsided and been replaced by fear, real fear.

'My job is to protect important people from dangerous and ungrateful people like you. There are people who are having to work hard to keep things going in this country. If it weren't for us, would you be able to enjoy the calm you have at your office, your home? Would you?'

Billy knew that this was an invitation for him to answer. He felt totally dominated and dwarfed by this giant. He could only guess that this must be the famous, no – correction – the notorious, Kaka – who, it was common knowledge, had made his way to the very top in the police force through his brutality. It was alleged that any dirty job that needed doing was done by him: dirty jobs, clean-finish jobs, irrational jobs, carefully planned jobs – any job. His price was high and he got it. If he wanted to go to America, he went, Russia, he went. He drove a BMW. Nobody knew his name except that he was Kaka. Rumour also had it that Kaka was his childhood nickname and those who propagated this rumour had the satisfaction of claiming knowledge of his humble origins – when the umbilical cord stub fell, who cleaned mucus from his nose, when he was initiated, how girls refused him and poked fun at his small head perching on disproportionately broad shoulders.

But now, if all that rumour had to crystallise in a real coldblooded mammal stamping its heavy feet on the helpless floor and letting its arms fly free all over the room, knocking off in their wake any obstacles, then fear had to register in Billy's eyes, mouth, and stomach. Consequently Billy's eyes moistened, his mouth went dry, and crickets started hopping around inside his stomach.

'Now that you can drive around in fancy cars,' the giant resumed, 'you have forgotten who paid for your education and gave you employment. Now you think you are the ones who have become masters, right? What kind of ingratitude is that – that you can actually bite the very hand that is scooping porridge into your mouth?'

'But sir…' he wasn't allowed to finish even this extremely unpalatable interjection. This time the blow was heavier and he went down, regretting instantly the use of *sir*. Can you really, he thought, call this miscreant *sir*, when all he deserves is a place in the rubbish dump? What was happening to this world that such monsters should be allowed to exert so much authority on fellow human beings in the name of purity? Hasn't this world seen enough examples of such misplaced trust? Is Hitler really too far back in history? Hasn't the third world seen enough examples of their own such monstrosities?

'Now you want a trial, eh?' Kaka asked sarcastically.

Billy stayed on the floor and when he looked at the unnerving heaving of the chest above him he started a prayer he wasn't allowed to finish. His only satisfaction was in starting a prayer his father would have prayed, in the same manner Baba would have started it. In his heart he realised how simple and humble he had always been and simply said, 'Dear God forgive me for I knew not what I was doing.'

He remembered the actual prayer Jesus prayed. But he failed to reconcile himself to the idea of forgiving 'them' for they all knew what they were doing. Billy had always loathed helplessness and self-pity. He now feared these two enemies winning as he felt the lump on his head and the blood flowing from his right eye. He saw Kaka walk out, but only vaguely. By this time Billy had decided he was going to change his prayer. 'Forgive me God for what I am about to do.' He wasn't going to court after all. But then he could not see himself with just one eye. Those who loved him must remain with Billy's whole image.

When morning came, Chimwemwe had already been allowed to breastfeed her baby boy, now five hours old. He had come two weeks early, but the doctor said it might have been due to miscalculations on his part. As she looked at the baby, she wondered whether he would have a father to raise him. For days now nobody had seen Billy. Mr Vubi had advised against panic. Khumbo had to write the commissioner for intervention. They were still waiting for an answer.

She went on to reflect on Baba's reaction to a first grandson. She had not met him since that fateful day when he had come to her father and called them heathen. Moslems had no place in heaven, he had said. She chuckled as she wondered whether Billy's son by a Moslem girl was anywhere nearer heaven. If she could influence events, she concluded, she would call him Shaibu as a seal of his future dedication to Islam.

The door opened and Mai Nabanda walked in carrying a basket.

'How is my little husband,' she teased the baby who was sucking away and lying contentedly on his mother's lap.

'Answer, you greedy man,' Chimwemwe joined her in the teasing.

'Now if you want to grow to be as big as your father, that's the way to eat. Boy did he eat.'

They laughed.

'Talking about his father,' Mai Nabanda started, 'I don't like the dreams I have been having lately.'

Chimwemwe looked down at the baby and her whole body froze. The baby let the breast slip from his mouth and did not cry. She always feared Mai Nabanda's dreams. She had predicted it would be a boy. And here he was.

'Have you ever heard of your husband going hunting?'

Chimwemwe looked at her with blank eyes.

'Well, in this dream he goes hunting and then a group of people bring back an antelope on a stretcher. Except for the head the rest of the body is human. And he is not in the group.'

'Has Khumbo heard from the commissioner?' Chimwemwe asked.

'They say he is out of the country.'

Silence. When Chimwemwe looked at the baby, he had fallen asleep. Shaibu was beautiful in his sleep.

* * *

Khumbo was revving up the engine. The time was 7 o'clock. He turned to look at the hotel where days had rolled into weeks, with Sue having the best of times by the swimming pool or walking around the city streets. As for him, every minute he had spent with Sue had proved rewarding – emotionally and otherwise. His financial position had improved with the Ministry's decision to accommodate him in the hotel while a house was being sought for him. He was now coming to grips with the situation at the General Hospital: congested wards, a general shortage of drugs, and long outpatient queues.

On the whole he was grateful to Sue for not bringing up for discussion anything pertaining to their future. He needed all the time to handle Billy's problem. His father's presence at Sam's house had been a source of embarrassment, especially with his mother staying on to witness both the birth of Shaibu and the outcome of Billy's case. Baba had agreed to extract himself from the scene mostly because Khumbo had no house of his own. Sam had tried to intervene by offering to keep him for as long as it took to resolve Billy's problem. But he had argued differently and opted to return home and go back to work. And he had gone back: not a word had he exchanged with his ex-wife, not a word with his daughter-in-law. Khumbo had driven him back.

He engaged reverse gear and pulled out of the parking space. He then methodically engaged first gear and was about to let the car roar away when he saw Sue in the rear-view mirror running towards the car. He stopped the car and waited for her to get to the window.

'There's something you must see,' she said.

'What?' he asked, more concerned by her look than by what she was saying. Her face had gone pale.

'Come back inside.'

He opened the door.

'No, park the car first.'

He did as he was told and got out. Sue was already seven steps ahead of him so that the distance between them ruled out any possibility of conversation. He followed her past the reception desk. It was amazing how busy the hotel reception desk was at that early hour. When he got to the room Sue was in tears, looking out through the window.

'What is it?' he asked.

'The paper,' she said without turning.

He turned round to look at the bed where the bold letters gazed at him with the mockery of Lucifer in the garden of Eden after Adam and Eve had fallen from grace:

DRUG DEALER HANGS HIMSELF IN GAOL

He didn't read any further. He slumped into a chair and looked at Sue without seeing her, for his eyes were crystal with water. Anger welled up inside him as he locked his ten fingers and cracked them several times over. Sue came to him and sat on the armrest and put her arm around his neck. She held herself against him as she sobbed freely. Khumbo was grateful for her presence.

Minutes ticked away and they didn't talk. After a while Sue was able to recall the first paragraph of the story:

> A civil servant being held on remand after being denied bail was found dead last night. He is Mr Billy Dala who was found hanging from a roof. He had used a necktie...

She didn't want to remember any more.

'Khumbo,' she called in a whisper.

He turned to look up at her.

'Mai Nabanda... Somebody has to be there when she gets the news!'

Khumbo was back on his feet in no time.

'You better stay here,' he instructed.

'I am coming with you.'

'No, you are not!'

'I am and I'm driving.

She ended up driving, giving Khumbo a chance to plan his next move. Baba had to be told and collected. His views on the place of burial had to be consulted. Ellen and Paweme had to be told. He would ask Sam to do it on his behalf.

His mother had already heard. The screaming and wailing could be heard half a mile away. By the time they arrived the house was already teeming with women. Mai Nabanda and Chimwemwe had already been assigned women to look after them and control them. It was not uncommon for women to threaten to kill themselves and follow their husbands, fathers, sons, etc. Nobody has allowed the experiment to be carried out to see whether or not that would actually happen. There were always sufficient women to plead with the bereaved in their times of sorrow, always persuading them that much as they shared the tragedy it was important to see a light at the end of the tunnel.

When the car stopped he hesitated and in that moment he caught phrases from Mai Nabanda and Chimwemwe which pierced him right to his heart. Mai Nabanda was loudest.

'My son. Who'll look after me? Why leave me alone?'

Chimwemwe's was a typical widow's lament: 'Why did you have to be so selfish? Who'll look after your son? Why leave him fatherless? At least you could have seen him. Why can't I do anything right?'

There were many other women who used the occasion to remember their own misfortunes. In crying, they were more concerned about their past losses than Mai Nabanda's or Chimwemwe's. The whole thing sounded strange to Sue. The number of mourners already gathered, their level of emotional involvement – it all left her wondering how she, a prospective daughter-in-law, was supposed to conduct herself.

Khumbo stepped down from the car and walked towards the house. He was met by Sam who held him by the arm and led him into the house. Once inside he sat close to his mother and cried openly and loudly. Chimwemwe was lying on the mat and had two women attending to her. After a while he walked out to join Sam.

'Ellen and Paweme read about it in the paper,' Sam said. 'They are coming.'

'Somebody has to tell Baba.' Khumbo suggested.

'He knows.'

'I guess I have to go and get him,' Khumbo said.

'I've already sent the Golf. He should be here by noon.'

'I appreciate that, Sam.'

'He was a brother to me,' Sam couldn't help shedding a tear.

Billy's body was laid to rest the following day at the City Council cemetery without any religious ceremony. He hadn't been to church for years and therefore no clergy would allow members of his church even to sing hymns. This was Baba's biggest blow. As soon as he had recovered from the initial shock, Baba had taken his rightful role as head of the family and he and Khumbo went about organising the funeral, with Sam as their right hand.

Upon advice from Mr Vubi, the coffin could only stay in the house for up to two hours. Mr Vubi further advised them not to open the coffin for viewing as he had been well informed about the body's condition. Mr Vubi had grounds to suspect foul play in Billy's death and was willing to pursue the matter with the authorities if the family so wished.

'What chances are there that it wasn't suicide?' Khumbo asked.

'Fifty-fifty. And that's a pretty high percentage either way.'

'What do you think, Baba?' Khumbo asked.

'I feel very angry about it all,' Baba said. 'What you must consider is whether this thing that has hit us has potential to hurt us further. What about Mr Vubi's practice? Answers to these worries should guide us, not anger.'

'Mr Vubi, what do you think is the right thing to do?' Khumbo asked.

'Baba is right,' Mr Vubi answered. 'I am convinced we haven't got the whole story here. But do we really want to do it Billy's way? How long do we want to fight? What kind of victory are we looking for? I couldn't help Billy when he was alive. I am not too sure I could help him now. If I did it, it would be because I have been hurt by his death which I couldn't do anything to prevent. And still, I have to ask myself whether even that is enough reason to fight.'

'All right,' Khumbo started. 'None of this should be uttered to the women. When all is over they will ask awkward questions. None of these suspicions should be disclosed.

By noon the house was teeming with people. Paweme and Ellen arrived by Express and were collected by Sam. Upon their entry into the house there was a fresh wave of wailing and screaming. Sue had by now observed that the coming in of any relation was a starting point of fresh wailing, the intensity of which varied with the closeness of the new arrival to the deceased. The new arrival herself (women were by far the loudest) was the dominant performer at the time.

Sue had also observed that by noon half the women were busy making fires and cooking. Most women donated maize flour, beans, and other forms of food. But most food had been gathered by Party officials who had gone round the location seeking assistance. After twenty years of independence the Party had established itself as a strong – if not the strongest – social welfare organisation, certainly only second, if at all, to the church movement. It was responsible for organising celebrations, it assisted at weddings and took over most funerals. This Party participation was most welcome as it left Khumbo and Baba enough time to look after the coffin and cemetery arrangements.

The biggest incident, which Sue would never forget, took place when the Nkhotakota team arrived. That the Dalas had lived almost all their lives in Nkhotakota was evidenced by the arrival of two overcrowded trucks from that town. They had responded to the news of their district commissioner's bereavement with shock and oneness, both of which they had come to display fervently. As a government officer he was entitled to certain privileges such as transport, and this had taken the form of a truck. But the citizens of Nkhotakota would not be satisfied with just getting on the truck. They were going to add to that. So that nobody complained of being left behind for lack of space the Nkhotakota Party officials had organised the gathering into hiring an additional one. Further to that five goats were donated, two by the Asian community, three by the rest. By the time all the donations had been assembled, the team had to show for their efforts seven baskets of maize flour, a basket of beans, five goats, and K50.00 cash.

Disembarking from the trucks was the opposite of all these elaborate preparations. Women were clamouring to get out, each one contesting the front position in displaying their emotions and convincing Baba and Mai Nabanda of their closeness to the tragedy. The Party chairman sought out Baba and expressed his condolences. Everyone on the truck took his turn until they had all said their bit.

'Baba', that's what everybody called him. And so Nankhuni the Party chairman addressed him in the same manner.

'Baba, I was not there when the news broke out. So, John, my youngest, ran two miles non-stop. Two miles non-stop to deliver the message. *"Atate,"* he said, "All is not well in town." I said, "What is it now, my son?" "It's Baba," he said.'

'"Billy has left us!" I dropped my hoe and stood there for I don't know how long. The boy wouldn't say what had happened. But when I recovered from the shock, I ran home to get the people organised. I ran two miles non-stop.' He paused as he fished out an envelope.

'Baba' he continued,' we are together in this tragedy.'

'Those are kind words *a*Nankhuni.'

'Here, the people of Nkhotakota would like you to accept this little collection to assist with the funeral.'

'Words fail me *a*Nankhuni. May God bless you all.'

'You have been a father to us. *A*Billy was our brother. The way we have known him, I am sure he deserved a more honourable death.'

'Well,' Baba said, a tear rolling from his left eye, 'Billy has died like a dog. Not even a last wish.'

'Baba, let's take solace in God almighty who sees all, knows all, and was with him when he departed from this earth. Come with me, Baba, there are things in the car. We have to feed these people.'

'You are most generous. I will take you to the area Party chairman who is in charge of receiving and organising food.' The two men went round the house and the handover took place as efficiently as Baba would have handled it himself. The goats were slaughtered and gigantic aluminium pots were throbbing with heat in record time.

At the graveyard Baba took everybody by surprise when he stood up as soon as the coffin had been lowered into the grave.

'Let us pray,' he said.

There was a wave of whispering and the clergy exchanged angry glances. But Baba did not wait for quiet to return.

'My dear God in heaven,' he started in a croaky and broken voice. 'I appeal to you to be the only one to judge my son – your son. Do not allow us sinful mortals to judge Billy. We were not with him in his last moments. His last words were to you my God, not to me, a pastor, a reverend, or a bishop. He talked to you before surrendering his soul. I beg you to judge him like you judged your children before him. I beg you to receive his soul. If we sang songs here, said prayers, and preached sermons, my God, these would not have influenced your judgement.

'My humble prayer is that you teach us not to judge here on earth for we shall be judged by the same measurement when we leave this world. Judge Billy as he deserves, dear God. I ask this in the name of your son Jesus Christ. Amen.'

'Amen,' the crowd chorused.

The wailing from Mai Nabanda, Chimwemwe, Paweme and Ellen was even louder after prayer. The other women felt forced to join them as the burial proceeded.

As they walked from the cemetery Mr Vubi held Khumbo by the hand and led him aside. He was already breathing heavily as a result of the walking. Khumbo was now running out of ideas as to how best to warn these so-called prosperous Malawians that there were healthier ways of demonstrating their success in life. Certainly over-indulgence wasn't one he would recommend.

'By the way, heads have started to roll after all,' Mr Vubi said between gasps.

'What do you mean?' Khumbo by now found the subject of Billy's activities disconcerting, although he was interested in the new developments.

'I didn't want to tell you earlier. Until all this was over. Inspector Chinangwa has been arrested in Zimbabwe. At Harare Airport.'

'When?'

By now they had stopped, letting the throng of mourners pass them on their way home. This, of course, offered Mr Vubi much needed respite.

'Yesterday. Interpol. The whole thing seems to have been well investigated.'

Khumbo could only afford a sigh of disgust.

'There will be more arrests,' Mr Vubi confided further. 'The Government is very upset. The least you can expect is some dismissals from the force.'

'Will there be a trial then?'

'I think so. And that's the worst part. Your mother.'

'Oh, no!'

'I am almost certain about that, whether or not the Zimbabwe government decides to extradite Chinangwa. At the moment they need him for their own purposes.' He paused as if not to proceed. Khumbo's stare and furrowed forehead, however, disarmed him totally and he proceeded.

'It involves some important names in Zimbabwe as well, and his testimony is crucial in their trial. Chinangwa was not alone when they arrested him. He had a Zimbabwean counterpart.'

'What concrete evidence have they got against them?' Khumbo's concern was seeing the culprits in for the longest term possible. Especially if Mai Nabanda was going in as well.

'They were both leaving for Johannesburg and were in possession of *mandrax* and *chamba*.'

'Let's go,' Khumbo said disgustedly. By now the street was quiet. Most people had dispersed and gone to their respective homes. Some would be stopping at their favourite pubs, others at their friends' homes. Life would go on as usual, Khumbo observed.

'By the way,' Khumbo couldn't let this go untouched. 'Will it be possible to link Billy's death to these arrests?'

'That's the saddest part,' Mr Vubi said, shaking his head. 'That won't be possible.'

'Why not – he wanted a trial and, as far as we know, died in search of it, if not because of it.'

'It's precisely that which we can't prove. Especially now that Chinangwa is Zimbabwe's principal prosecution witness, I don't see him as of much use to us from there. All Billy managed to do was implicate his mother in the charge against him. Now she can't get out.'

'So here ends the story of Billy Dala, without conclusion.'

'I am afraid so. But then here starts another whose conclusion we can't guess. Hardly the best result, but Billy would have settled for nothing less than these arrests.'

Still, Khumbo could only shake his head in disgust at the seeming futility of his brother's death.

Chapter Eight

When Grace approached Khumbo to offer her condolences and bid him farewell, Sue was there, sitting next to him. This was the day after the burial, just before the last ceremony to be conducted according to custom which freed the mourners, particularly the distant bereaved, (cousins, uncles, etc.) from hanging around the premises. This meeting mostly took place on the morning following the burial. Referred to as *kusesa bwalo*, the ceremony is best described as the sweeping of the ashes which have accumulated over the days and evenings from fires made for cooking and, particularly, those around which the male folk spent their nights. This vigil is part of the last respects paid to the deceased.

Grace would have preferred to meet him on his own, but Sue wouldn't let Khumbo out of her sight. Sue watched her approach, her unsteady steps well disguised in the *chirundu* in which she had wrapped herself. One thing Sue had learnt to use fast was the *chirundu*, since every woman came to the funeral wrapped in one. It was a means of making up for the shortness of a dress or a skirt. But more than that, it allowed every woman a certain degree of modesty and humility at a time when a flashy dress (certainly a short one) would have been misconstrued. As a result secretaries, teachers, nurses, all assumed humble stature wrapped in a *chirundu* and with their heads in a *doek*, an equally popular and functional headdress. Grace had much to tell him but she had to be content with a handshake.

'You must know, Doctor, how deeply affected we all are,' she said, kneeling across the water drain. Sue and Khumbo were sitting with their backs against the wall and their legs in the drain.

'I thank you for your kind words,' Khumbo said in the same formal vein, unable to look her straight in the eye.

'I haven't been able to speak to Baba and Mai Nabanda. Tell them I share with them this moment of loss.' Before leaving a funeral gathering, it was always considered prudent to look up the widow or widower, or any other person close to the deceased, in order to say a few words of encouragement.

'On their behalf, I thank you for your kindness.'

'I must go now,' she said standing up, her legs dragging an unwilling and jealous heart. If only she could tell him…

'I will see you off,' Khumbo said as he stood up. 'By the way, this is my fiancée Sue. Sue, this is Grace, a friend.'

Grace offered her hand for a handshake but Sue just called out 'How do you do?' Grace silently congratulated herself for tearing up the note without reading it. This man had swallowed the bait and the hook and Sue had come out the winner.

As they walked away towards the road where the car was parked, Sue watched helplessly while debating whether to join them or not.

'He'll come back,' she said to herself and leaned against the wall again, green with envy, struggling with the urge to take her on, whoever this 'Grace friend' was.

It was only after the car had gathered speed on the road to the bus depot that Grace sighed with relief. Until that moment she was expecting Sue to pounce on her or at least jump into the car with them.

'Whew! My, my, my. You really are being guarded jealously.'

'What did you expect?' Khumbo replied.

'I don't believe she has actually let you go.'

'Well, she has.'

'And with me for that matter.'

'Sue doesn't know anything…'

They drove in silence, Khumbo deliberately ignoring the unwelcome hints from Grace who would have preferred to discuss Sue further.

'I've just said yes to a marriage proposal,' Grace said on a more serious note.

'Impossible! Why?' Khumbo's turn had come to feel the pangs of jealousy.

'Why not?' she challenged aggressively.

'Who is he?' Khumbo was relentless in his frustration.

Grace didn't answer.

'Grace,' Khumbo said seriously. 'I don't want you to marry him.'

'Oh, yah,' she said sarcastically.

'I mean it. You said he didn't love you.'

'What has love got to do with it? What makes you think I'd tell you everything about him?'

Grace didn't say anything more until they reached the bus depot. Khumbo tried to talk her into thinking seriously again about her future.

When they got to the depot she took her bag from him with the left hand and extended her right.

'You had to go, just like that,' she said tearfully. 'You don't know how I'll miss you.' Khumbo was speechless as he mustered all his bravery to refrain from looking at her eyes, for his were flooded as well. He should have hugged her in the car, a quick kiss or something. But now what could he do in this crowd? They squeezed each other's hand for some time and she turned to get on the bus. It was a Blantyre bus.

Khumbo waited until she had found a seat, which was at the window. He walked to her and extended his hand just to touch her again.

'You didn't tell me you were going to Blantyre?' he queried.

'I think I am going to have a baby,' she whispered evasively, and a tear or two landed on Khumbo's hand.

So thunderstruck was Khumbo that he clung to her

hand squeezing it until it hurt. He had nothing to say to her, and they both knew it.

'Are you certain?' he gasped, helpless.

'I'm hoping Dan won't find out,' she whispered, as if the man sitting next to her was her father-in-law. 'I need a father for my baby,' she continued as she cried openly. 'I'll just have to accept his proposal.'

'Listen, am I… you mean I am…'

She pulled her hand away and sat down, closing the window as she did so, furious that he could even have doubted his role in the matter.

'Get down, Grace,' he shouted, but she wouldn't even look at him.

'Come down and we'll talk.' Even as he shouted to her, he knew he had nothing more to say to her, not a promise, not commitment. His mind was a whirlwind.

He ran round the door hoping to get in. The bus was so full the conductor wasn't letting in any more passengers. Good heavens! He needed time to think things through. And these women were pushing too hard.

'I am not a passenger,' Khumbo pleaded. 'I want to see somebody on the bus.'

The conductor pressed the bell and Khumbo was forced to run back to the window. The window was open but a man was sitting there now. He tried to look for her but all he saw was a mass of black faces as the bus gathered speed.

He watched the bus disappear past the Lilongwe market and round the corner to join the Blantyre road, billows of dust forming at the edge of the tarmac as it gathered speed.

'Damn it,' he cursed himself as he walked to the car, wondering how time could have passed so fast; how a mere two months could breed so many complications to the point of snatching the reins from his hitherto firm grip. And how he didn't know any more who was controlling his life – whether his fate was being controlled from heaven or hell.

As he approached the junction, swallowing the dust thrown up by the bus, he toyed with the idea of turning right to follow the bus in the hope that he could catch up with it before the next bus stop. But the state of the Renault convinced him of the futility of such an attempt. Grace's revelation was ill timed to say the least. He turned left at the end of Market Road into Kamuzu Procession Road, back to area 18, resolving to worry about Grace later. Now that he was on his own again, he wondered how it was so easy to start a family without proper planning. He was used to women taking precautions and having babies only when they were ready to have them. And he was such a man, too, one who prided himself with being in control of his own destiny.

As he turned into area 18 his mind was clearer. Nobody, not even Grace nor Sue, nor Mai Nabanda for that matter, was going to control his destiny. Never again would he let his fate be decided by other people, Baba, Sue, or even those yet to be born. He was a man in control of his fate, and that resolution gave him the much-needed respite as he prepared himself for the forthcoming *kusesa bwalo*.

When he returned to the house the ceremony was about to begin. Breakfast had already been served so that anyone who didn't feel a part of this ceremony was already leaving. In fact everybody had already turned up except him. He was invited in and shown a place very close to his maternal uncle, Jumbe. Baba sat in one corner to his left and Mai Nabanda sat on his right next to Chimwemwe. Both ladies and Paweme and Ellen wore black head-dress. Sue was not in the room.

'Where is Sue?' Khumbo whispered to Paweme, without being sure whether he was ready to meet her yet. What would he tell her?

'She went for a walk.'

'Which way?'

'Up the road,' Paweme said. 'You are not going anywhere. These people have been waiting for you.'

'For me?'

'Well, my friends,' Uncle Jumbe addressed the gathering as if to shut Khumbo up.

'It is time for us to thank you and release you so that you can go home.'

There followed a minute of shuffling, coughing, and summing up, little gossip stories, etc., in preparation for the more substantial discussions ahead. Khumbo remembered his confrontation with the three craftsmen on his way to Nkhotakota and sat down proudly. The bearded Uncle Jumbe now occupied centre stage. His beard reminded Khumbo of Billy's. In fact, how much Billy had taken after him, Khumbo thought. Many were making a similar comparison from various corners of the room.

'Help me to put things right in this family,' Uncle Jumbe started again. This was the time when differences were analysed and affected parties requested to reconcile. 'The young man who has left us was the pillar on which these three women – I mean four – depended.' He was pointing a finger at Mai Nabanda, Chimwemwe, Paweme and Ellen.

'There are two men left now: Baba and the doctor here. We all know that Baba is now weak and also that he really does not consider these women his responsibility any more...'

'We must be careful what we say here,' Uncle Nkeka butted in. He was Baba's elder brother, and had never been known to mince words. Mai Nabanda had not forgotten the coarse tongue that had lashed at her once.

'Let us stick to instructions and avoid opening old wounds.'

There was a wave of murmurs of approval.

'I am sorry if I seem to be opening old wounds here,' Jumbe replied. 'But that's the way it has to be. Many people here don't know the history of the family.'

'And they don't have to know,' Nkeka interjected. 'So

get on to the main issue. In any case, who chose you to preside over these discussions? Fellow elders, for these discussions to be conducted properly, I suggest the Party chairman of this area should preside.'

Everybody supported the motion and the chairman made himself known at once.

'We will not dwell on matters that will split the family,' the chairman started.

'But the family is already split...' Jumbe wouldn't let that point be dismissed.

'In what way?'

'These children's parents are divorced – have been for the past three... four years. And, Mr Chairman, that is very important.'

'Yes, I see your point,' the chairman said. He then turned to Nkeka. 'This man has a valid point. Let us settle that one first. Who has had custody of the children?'

'The mother,' Jumbe answered.

'So it is your problem really – your *mbumba* in every sense of the word.'

'I am glad you can now see my point of view.'

Nkeka was silent this time.

'Fellow elders and friends, the picture is now clearer. Let me ask Jumbe, therefore, to bear with us as we assist him with his problem. I suggest that the old man, the father, deserves as much of our attention as these ladies here.'

'Mr Chairman,' an unknown gentleman butted in. 'That is a valid point. Like you said earlier, we should not dwell on matters that will split the family further. That man there is old and needs help. He is the father of *malemu*. We cannot change that. If there were any differences between him and *malemu*, this is the time to forget them.'

The speaker had the whole gathering on his side. '*A*Jumbe,' the chairman said. 'What these people would want to assist with is whether the deceased has left any property which might be a source of problems in the family. It is those here who don't stand to gain anything who can reason out objectively and suggest solutions. And, second, there is the matter of the child and the widow. She will need our guidance. So can you introduce us to your *mbumba* and then address the questions before us so that we can proceed.'

Jumbe cleared his throat, happy that he could influence the trend of the discussions again.

'Thank you *a*Chairman. I'll start with the widow here and then the mother, and the two ladies here are the only girls in the family. The doctor here is the eldest. In the corner there is my brother-in-law, the father of the children. The man with whom I have exchanged words already happens to be my fellow *nkhoswe*. He represents Baba's side and I Mai Nabanda's every time matters affecting this family spring up. I think that's enough of an introduction.

'Now coming to what the *malemu* has left behind.'

'Mr Chairman,' Khumbo interrupted. 'This won't be necessary as the deceased left a will. I suggest the will be read to the members of the family at the appropriate time.' He was impatient to wind up the discussions as he had his own personal life to sort out.

'That simplifies matters,' the chairman said. 'We will move on to consider other matters.'

'What will?' Nkeka asked, perplexed, at the same time voicing the worries and mistrust of many. 'What is this will business, *a*Chairman?'

'I also agree with my counterpart,' Jumbe joined in. 'This is Malawian practice and we should not bring in English words to confuse each other. Tradition demands that we look at what our son had and then we would see how best to distribute the things.'

There was a split in the gathering: the elders on one side, suspicious of the younger generation on the other. They would not let the young get away with their tricks. A general commotion ensued. Khumbo felt awkward and responsible for the chaos. But he believed he had as much right as anybody in the group to air his views, especially if they led to a speedy conclusion of the meeting.

'Wait a minute,' the chairman had to shout to be heard. 'Listen to me, all of you. This young man has not said anything outrageous. Modern practice allows that a man declares in writing how his fortunes are to be distributed. There is nothing complicated about that. If some of you have never heard of such practices, I am telling you now. All I want now is verification of Dr Khumbo's statement.'

He turned to Khumbo.

'How do we know you are not trying to get away with everything?'

'Mr Vubi is here and he is the lawyer in whose custody my brother left the will.'

'It is true, Mr Chairman,' Mr Vubi confirmed. 'And the instructions are that his father also be present if he so wished.' He so wished.

'What about me?' Jumbe jumped to his feet. 'What wrong did we do him?'

'I don't know about you,' Nkeka said. 'But my brother's children never came to see us. I am not surprised at what is taking place here. They have all been strangers to us.' Baba winced as it was his manner of bringing up children which was now facing judgement.

'This is what people are here to help you sort out,' the chairman stepped in. 'These people are here to seek an understanding with your children. Am I not right, elders?'

'You are, *a*Chairman,' the Party secretary said.

'We know these differences exist in all families. You are not an exception. We are here to intercede on behalf of the part that feels wronged or left out.' He paused.

'Those were the very words in my mouth, *a* Chairman,' the secretary continued. 'This is not the first funeral we have attended. But our elders decided to have such meetings as these to serve that very purpose. Let me appeal to these young ones. Your will is going to say a lot of things. We won't be there. But whatever it says, remember these elders here who are walking in rags. Help them out of their shame. These patches they are wearing should be your embarrassment, your shame…'

'Those are words of wisdom,' somebody shouted from the floor.

'Heed them, my children,' another remarked.

'I also want to speak, *a*Chairman.' This was a lady Khumbo had never met before. 'I know the family very well. I carried the doctor on my back when he was that high. But the saddest story is that the family has broken up the way it has. Just look at their father. Does he look like one who has a doctor and secretaries for children?'

'Not at all,' said one from the gathering.

'Tell them, Nangozo,' said another, a lady.

'If I look haggard,' she continued, 'it is because my children never saw the value of school. Well, perhaps I didn't either. But that was my fate. But for a man who saw into the future and had his children properly prepared for it, it is embarrassing that only the mother should look as well as she does. Who can believe that she is the ex-wife of Baba?'

There was a murmur of embarrassment, particularly among the men.

'No, you answer me. I am not known for beating about the bush. If I don't speak up now where else shall I get the chance?'

'Speak now, Nangozo.'

'You speak for everyone.'

Nangozo continued: 'Who said children should take sides when their parents fight? Who?'

'It is unheard of.'

'Who said children should not...'

'Wait a minute,' Jumbe interrupted. 'I don't know you or where you come from. Who gives you authority to speak as if you are the *nkhoswe* in the family?'

'*Bambo* Jumbe,' the chairman intervened. 'If the *ankhoswe* decide to spend their time quarrelling over money and fortunes, then let those with eyes speak. This lady is saying the things you or your counterpart should be saying. Am I not right?'

'You are, *a*Chairman,' somebody shouted.

'*A*Jumbe should sit down. He himself needs to be guided in these matters – in spite of his age.'

'*Bambo*,' the chairman took over. 'I suggest you sit down. This lady is a respectable member of the community here and she claims to know the family well. And she is here as part of this gathering. Those are enough reasons why she should speak. Unless, of course, you want this thing to be handled entirely as a family matter.'

'In which case he will be the first to conclude funeral matters in that manner in our history.'

'Why can't he just sit down. Does he want the car?'

'Why not ask for it properly then?'

Jumbe's legs sagged and he threw himself down.

'Thank you, Mr Chairman and friends, for supporting me.' Nangozo started again. 'I was going to make one last point and here it is: if we guide these children into loving their father the way they love their mother, they will be able to love their uncles and aunts as well. If children have no feeling for their father, they are animals. Is it any wonder then that the uncles are going about in rags? I'll sit down, Mr Chairman.'

'Mr Chairman,' a man spoke from near Baba. 'The father of these children would like to speak.'

'Let him speak.'

'I don't have much to say except to thank you for what you are saying to correct the children and us parents. But my worry is not with us old ones. We are already wasted. My worry is with my daughter-in-law.'

At this point everyone turned to face him. Chimwemwe's heart missed a beat.

'That girl is still young. She has hardly come out of *chikuta* and this tragedy hits her. You offer her a word of consolation, a word of advice.'

'Well spoken, *mdala*,' someone spoke with a Zimbabwean accent. 'It's time we looked at the real matters. How do we help the widow organise her life again? This thing has happened early in her life. She now has to raise the child on her own. Mr Chairman, *mdala* there has grabbed the bull by the horns. He needs assistance in controlling it.'

'*A*Chairman,' Jumbe raised his voice. 'Allow me to speak as the owner of the *mbumba*. If I go wrong correct me. Within our system we have a way of taking care of our widows. Our son had a brother who is with us here. Are the days gone when he would have been the natural choice to look after his brother's widow and child?'

There was total silence, mostly from fear as to what reaction this suggestion would provoke from Khumbo, who just sat mute, rooted to his place on the floor by the suddenness of this eventuality. The stars in his eyes flashed crazily as he made efforts to keep steady at the helm of his destiny.

'Yes. Are those days gone?' He eyed everybody challengingly.

'Would you call it primitive?'

The chairman cleared his throat. 'Now that the question is here with us, let us help each other in trying to arrive at a solution.'

Nobody, not even Baba, had expected this turn of events. When Baba suggested the subject of the widow, it was because the will or inheritance was being discussed in terms of the parents, brothers, sisters, or uncles; never in terms of Chimwemwe and the child. Now that Jumbe had started along this new line, Baba wondered who in the room had the audacity or his rustic wisdom to stand up to him.

'I have asked a question,' Jumbe continued. 'And I get no answer. I will ask another one. Is it too early to ask such a question?'

'No!' several elderly people chorused.

'Let's get on with the question then.'

'Ask the owners,' one suggested.

'Their feelings...'

'In fact, are you going to ask the doctor to take a

second wife?' asked another, tackling a dimension which Khumbo would have preferred to handle alone. Certainly if he was going to get help, this wasn't going to be the forum to provide it. The issue of marriage was being hurried, as far as he was concerned. But he must keep a cool head until the ship had sailed through the stormy waters.

'Is he already married?'

'He is. To a white.'

'We have a problem, then.'

The chairman cleared his throat to draw attention to himself. For a while he himself was confused by the details of the case as revealed by the unguided conversation.

'You have all raised good questions. To sum up, our major concern is the widow and the child. Agreed. Second, traditionally, Dr Khumbo Dala should be willing to take his brother's widow and therefore raise his nephew, now his son. The question now comes to the doctor. Are you going to do it or are you already married as some have suggested?'

'He can afford a second wife,' someone shouted from one corner.

The fury with which Khumbo was struggling inside in answering this question was beyond the imagination of any other member of the gathering. What amazed him more – indeed infuriated him – was the misinterpretation of Baba's innocent and genuine concern for Chimwemwe and her child, itself a very surprising gesture from the hitherto seemingly unforgiving and unforgetting old man, to suit their own selfish ends.

In response however he simply said: 'My elders, before I answer your question, I must echo my father's word of gratitude for offering us assistance during this most trying moment. Your questions are justified and they require an answer.'

Chimwemwe didn't know what to expect from Khumbo. So dazed was she by the occasion she couldn't tell when she might act improperly. She prayed to Allah that Khumbo would say the right things. She herself could not sort things out, so much so that she wondered how women in the villages handled such situations as these.

'There are two sides to my answer,' Khumbo continued. 'First, and most important, are the feelings of my *mlamu*. She has just lost a husband. Do we really expect her to think of a replacement now?'

'The coward,' Mai Nabanda muttered to herself. 'Just like the father.'

'It doesn't happen that way, son.'

The Zimbabwean accent was back. 'In principle, she has to indicate her willingness to go along with the suggestion. Then things are formalised later. We are not children, my son. Is that not so, *mdala*?'

'You are right,' the chairman said. 'But let him continue.'

'Thank you for the clarification. Now to the second part of my answer.' He felt the eyes on him, Baba's, Mai Nabanda's, Chimwemwe's, everybody's. But now these eyes didn't matter any more. He was still at the helm and negotiating the last mile of storm. By now he had learnt to use this explanation and it came as naturally as a 'hello'. After all it offered him the respite he now needed badly.

'I am married.' There was total silence; if a pin had dropped it would have burst somebody's eardrums. 'The white lady you have been seeing around is my wife. And I don't intend to marry a second wife. I hope I have answered your questions, my elders.'

Chimwemwe's tears flowed freely. For some reason she felt rejected for the second time by the same man to whom she had first surrendered her heart. But this rejection had greater impact because of the audience.

'Thank you, Doctor,' the chairman said. 'We have all heard for ourselves. What is left for me now is to refer the matter to Jumbe and Nkeka to choose the appropriate time, after the period of mourning is over, to "free" or *kunsudzula* Chimwemwe. But let me plead with her in-laws to allow her enough time to mourn her husband. Please do not act in haste. Are there any more points to raise?'

Mai Nabanda hated Baba even more for inflicting this final blow on Chimwemwe through his son.

There were no more points to raise.

'In that case let me thank you all for coming and assisting in this most important ceremony. Here in the city, it is important that we respond like this when death hits us the way it has done. On behalf of the party, the community and the family, I thank you. Please feel free to go.'

Khumbo was the first to go out in search of Sue. She was sitting on the *khonde* outside.

'Come with me,' he commanded, and she knew this was one of those times she had to follow without questioning. That distant look in his eyes said it all.

They got into the car and drove to the hotel. Once inside she didn't waste time:

'And now who is Grace?'

'Nobody,' he lied instinctively. He had been expecting the question and the answer was mechanical. 'Only Sue is everything.'

'Nonsense – a liar!'

'We are now man and wife, you understand?'

'Who are you fooling?'

'Listen, Sue. We have been passing for a married couple. All we need is a magistrate to formalise things.'

She was quiet.

'Yes or no?'

'I am not used to being rushed. Too many women around you.'

'If you weren't my wife, custom would demand that I marry Chimwemwe and take care of my brother's widow and child,' he threatened, very much playing the expediency game. He desperately needed this escape route.

'How preposterous! Would you?'

'You want to try me?'

'Of course not!' She rushed in to block that avenue

on remembering Chimwemwe's bewitching beauty. She immediately forgot Grace.

'Yes or no?'

'Yes! Yes! Yes! Let's get this straight though. We live together, like man and wife.'

'Yes…?' Khumbo was hesitant about the implication of this statement.

'We don't need a certificate.'

'I don't understand you,' Khumbo complained.

'But I don't understand you, either. And that's why I need more time.'

'Oh it's hopeless!' he sighed, the buzzes and stars returning to torment him.

'Those are my conditions. We go on as we have done before.'

'Yes,' he acquiesced dreamily. 'We'll go on as we have done.'

In spite of Mr Vubi's efforts to extricate Mai Nabanda from the wrath of the law for her involvement in Billy's drug trade, she still got what turned out to be a harsh sentence by all accounts. For complicity she got six months hard labour and had her import licence withdrawn. The farm which had been so instrumental in, to use the magistrate's words, the 'evil trade' was returned to tribal authorities for redistribution. Gona Pano Motel would be allowed to operate on condition that no *chamba* was smoked, grown, bought, or sold within two hundred metres of the motel. Similarly, trucks could operate on local licence only, the international one having been withdrawn indefinitely.

Before she was taken into the prison truck, Mai Nabanda asked for permission to talk to her son.

'*Achimwene*,' she said, her hardened eyes looking at him unflinchingly, as dry as he had known them to be at a wedding festival.

'You have a second chance to prove yourself a man.'

'What are you talking about, *mai*?'

'Two things,' she said. 'First, the business. There is a lot of life in that motel and in those trucks. Chimwemwe cannot manage on her own now that there is the little baby.'

'What can I do, mother? I work here in town. I can't supervise a business sixty miles away.'

'I can't tell you what to do. At your age, you should know what's right for you,' she said, and the hard eyes now softened and moistened. 'When you were far away and we were abandoned by your father, Billy had to make a decision.'

'But, mother...'

'He chose to look after his mother and sisters.'

'And Chimwemwe of course,' he added angrily.

'And Chimwemwe too. And he never regretted it.' Then she pointed a finger at him from her handcuffed hands, making it necessary to raise both arms.

'Shaibu will call you father whether or not you marry Chimwemwe. Because our ways demand that he does. And you will call him son. Because our ways demand that you do. Whether Billy lived to be a hundred years or not you two were meant to be father and son. That was the second thing I meant to tell you.'

As she was helped into the truck, she turned and said:

'I will need my business when I come back.'

The big doors were closed as noiselessly as the rusty hinges and the swinging chains could allow, imprinting on his memory a picture of his mother's helplessness which was to haunt him for the rest of her stay in prison. The truck roared away.

As Khumbo opened the passage door of the pick-up to let Chimwemwe get in his mind raced back to a couple of months ago, to what had seemed an innocent embarkation on a trip to Nkhotakota. Now he was retracing his steps in a prisoner role to deliver the very person he had hoped to surprise with his reappearance after eight years of absence. She was carrying baby Shaibu who soon demanded his feed, a demand she promptly met, thereby revealing the full and succulent breast. Khumbo caught himself envying his deceased brother this healthy and voracious heir to the Dala name. Chimwemwe had agreed to be driven home in the pick-up by Khumbo who would bring back the Golf and dispose of the Renault. He would then visit Gona Pano Motel at least once a fortnight to monitor the operation.

Khumbo's attempts at a conversation were a dismal failure. Chimwemwe did not feel bound to engage in verbal communication for anybody's convenience. Right now her preoccupation was the baby and the world disintegrating around him. She had brought forth a son to be part of a world she had helped build. As far as she was concerned Khumbo was just a fragment resulting from this cruel disintegration.

When he got home (they had by now been given a flat in area 11), Sue was ready for a real fight.

'And what does this mean?'

'What now?'

'You know very well what I mean.'

'I am tired,' he said as he slumped into a chair.

'The trial finished before noon, and this is past eight in the evening. How do you propose to explain that?'

'I had a lot of work to do,' he explained, rising to go to the fridge for his favourite beer. No offer was to be expected from Sue under the circumstances.

'What work? You just told me you were off duty. Why can't you tell me the truth for once?'

He was standing in the kitchen with a beer bottle which was already half-way down. He shook his head and it felt lighter. He was not ready to face the ferocious blue eyes and red face before him.

'I went to Salima,' he said coolly and took another substantial gulp.

'And what does that mean?' she gasped in a state of

shock. In her mind, the prayer repeatedly mocked her: oh God, not so soon!

'I went to the motel.'

'You mean you went to see your customary wife,' she ranted. 'Of course it's your social responsibility, etc. Oh cut it out. I've had enough of this.'

He opened the fridge again and brought out another 'green'. He expected more trouble at the rate things were going. He walked past her and sat down in his chair, making an effort not to let anger interfere with his confused and fatigued mind. He had to remain in control.

'It's the same magic name, isn't it?' She raved as she paced around the room. 'Chiwewe! Chiwewe! Chiwewe! She won't let go, will she?'

'You don't care, do you?' He asked her as placidly as his tired mind could.

'Care? Why should I care when I know I am being cheated? What…?'

'I've had the roughest day of my life. Mai Nabanda has just gone in for six months. She can only operate the motel and the truck business. Her farm has been forfeited. And I am the only man around.' He paused as he drained his first bottle, his furrows moistening in the full gaze of the disbelieving eyes in front of him.

'Instead of asking how my day has been, instead of finding out what has happened to my mother – *my mother* – you stand there and accuse me of things I haven't even dreamt of. I don't understand you. I don't know if I ever will.'

'Don't bother to make an effort. I am going. When I said no certificates I knew what I was talking about. I can't tell who is a friend and who isn't. And you won't help, either. These sisters, cousins, in-laws and what not! Everybody seems to be related to you. And now I have to sit here late hours waiting for you to return. Why can't somebody else be responsible for this mess? Why you? Why?'

He had told enough truth for the day. He needn't invite more trouble. What if she knew he had driven Chimwemwe and baby Shaibu to Salima from the court? What if he told her the briefcase he brought contained books of accounts and other documents on the motel? Suppose she knew that Chimwemwe would effectively be the manager of the business and he would have to drive to Salima every weekend to monitor events? And when she knew that he called Shaibu son because that's what your brother's son is to you, and Shaibu would call him father when he learnt to speak; if she knew all that, what would be left of the already strained relationship?

'You were such a great partner in London.' Khumbo said, defeated as he opened the second bottle.

'So were you, darling,' and she broke down as she rushed into Khumbo's arms. He had to be careful lest he spilled his beer. He squeezed her with one arm as he carefully placed the bottle on the window-sill with the other.

'Then why can't it work here?'

'I don't know,' she moaned.

As she clung helplessly to the man she loved so dearly,

all the fears she had had for months flashed through her mind with dizzying effect: the warnings she had heard about secret wives, dubious cousins, clans, or villages of dependants. When she arrived to find Chimwemwe married her fears had been allayed, but only until Billy's death. She had to admit Chimwemwe's beauty and dominance. Even as a pregnant woman she had posed a threat worse and more real than Grace. They had never exchanged a word; and now that her husband was gone feminine instinct told her that Chimwemwe was there to stay and fight. And the odds were in her favour. What chance did Sue have against her?

'I've never known you to be a loser,' Khumbo teased seriously.

She looked at him with her big eyes and somehow saw some truth in his statement.

'I've never been a loser,' she said firmly, not even allowing the water in her eyes to weaken her resolve.

'Khumbo Dala,' she said, her lips thinning into familiar determination.

'Yes, darling,' he answered on a similar serious note.

'This girl is a winner and she is here to stay.'

'That's my girl… I mean my wife.'

A Glossary of Chichewa Words

achimwene	brother
ada	an informal way of addressing a close male friend
aPhiri	a clan name used as a mark of respect, especially by a wife
atate	father
bamboo	father
Bo	slang for 'It's OK!' or 'I feel great'
bwana	sir
chamba	Indian hemp
chambo	a very popular tilapia dish, common in Malawi
chikuta	the period soon after birth when mother and child are kept in confinement
chirundu	traditional wrap-around used by women, worn breast-high
chitenje	a two-metre cotton material, commonly used by women as chirundu
doek	women's head-dress

gmelina	an exotic tree with broad leaves adapted to the tropics and used in afforestation projects
gumbagumba	a loud sound system used in bars for music
kanyenya	fried meat (chicken, fish, beef, pork, etc.), usually seasoned and hot
Kaya inu muli bwanji?	And how are you?
khonde	verandah
kunsudzula	the act of freeing a widow from her late husband's family so that she can remarry
kusesa bwalo	(a) literally, sweeping the yard or lawn (b) metaphorically, sweeping the ashes of fires around which mourners have kept vigil
mabvuto	problems
mai	mother
makola	herd
malemu	the deceased
mandrax	a form of drug in the opium class, sold and used illegally
manje	of Shona origin, mostly used by those who have lived in Zimbabwe
masese	dregs found at the bottom of a traditional beer container
masuku	a wild fruit

mbumba	sisters and children for whom a man is responsible
mdala	elder, elderly person (pl. – madala)
mlamu	in-law
mpiru	a popular vegetable used as a relish
Mulengi	Creator, God
Muli bwanji achimwene?	How are you, brother?
Mwadzuka bwanji, bwana?	How are you this morning, sir?
mzungu	white person
ncheni	a variety of tilapia fish found in Lake Malawi
Ndadzuka bwino kaya inu?	I'm fine this morning; how are you?
Ndiri bwino	I am fine
ng'anga	medicine man
nkhokwe	barn
nkhoswe	advocate (e.g., an uncle representing a boy or girl in marriage negotiations) (pl. – ankhoswe)
nkhuku	cockerel
nkhwani	a very popular vegetable dish of pumpkin leaves
nsima	a traditional dish made from maize, cassava or sorghum flour, accompanied by relish, vegetables, meat or gravy

nthudza	a wild fruit
shauliyako	That's your problem/It's none of my business
simanjemanje	A South African dance popular in the 1970s
timba	an African redbreast
utaka	a variety of tilapia fish found in Lake Malawi
zimalupsya	first rains. Literally, the rains that extinguish bushfires which are common in the dry season
zopusa zimenezo	That's silly/stupid

About the Author

JAMES NG'OMBE is a playwright and author born and educated in Malawi.

He completed his BA in English and History at the University of Malawi and went on to achieve an MSc from the University of Guelph, Canada, and a PhD from the University of London's Institute of Education. He lectured in Communication for nine years at the University of Malawi and currently works as Managing Director at Jhango Publishers.

Printed and bound by CPI Group (UK) Ltd, Croydon, CR0 4YY

20/03/2026

02075568-0001